Montmorency

Eleanor Updale

For Jim, Andrew
Catherine and Flora-Montmorency's
oldest friends

CONTENTS

1. 1875: THE BLOODY BEGINNING

The pain woke him again. Not the constant throb that was so familiar he could hardly remember being without it. This was one of those sharp stabs from the wound along his thigh. Doctor Farcett had dug deep to get through to the shattered bone, and the layers of catgut stitching pulled as the torn flesh struggled to realign itself inside. After so many interventions by the keen young medic, Montmorency should have been prepared for the agony, but each time the aftereffects seemed worse, and the limited pain relief (alcohol and the occasional treat of an experimental gas) less effective.

The candle on the central table had burned almost to nothing: It must be nearly morning, but there was no sign of light through the bars high up in the wall. Montmorency knew there was no point in calling for the night guard. Marston, silent, still, and unsmiling, saw his duties in the prison hospital as strictly limited to preventing escapes. Never mind the fact that Montmorency couldn't even turn over in bed, let alone run away. He'd have to wait in the dark for the arrival of Nurse Darnley, a brusque but well-meaning woman who believed that bad people could be made good and that providing a sip of water to a sick criminal might help that process.

In the meantime, as so often, Montmorency's memory threw up images from a year ago, of the night he was caught. He had hopped across the roof of the factory like an animal fleeing for its life. If he hadn't clung on to the bag of stolen tools, he might have seen the skylight window before his feet found it and he'd fallen through onto the hard iron frame of the grinding machine. He remembered the cold impact of metal against his skin, but nothing else until he'd heard people talking about him as if he wasn't there.

"I can assure you there will be no drain on hospital funds. I will provide all necessary equipment and supervision."

It was a voice he later recognized as that of Robert Farcett, the surgeon who wanted to make a name for himself by saving Montmorency from his multiple injuries.

Montmorency could only imagine what had happened in the interim. No doubt the police, finding his distorted body in the factory, had been delighted that he had gotten what he deserved for his crime. A quick death would save the courts the trouble and expense of dealing with him. But he had defied their expectations, and his mangled form had been carried off to the teaching hospital near the bridge, where Doctor Farcett had seen him for the first time. The injuries had been grievous, but the body around them had clearly been athletic and strong.

Farcett was preparing a paper for the Royal College of Surgeons on the treatment of complex wounds. He had considered traveling to the Balkans, to find casualties of war so that he could illustrate his theories with real examples. Now, as he worked late among the puking poor of London, an ideal subject lay before him. Without Farcett's help, the man would surely die. If he lived, Farcett's reputation might live on, too.

So it was that the relationship between the doctor and the pitiful heap of bloodstained clothing had developed into a project.

The creature didn't die. It survived long enough to become a man deemed fit to stand trial. He was charged under the name "Montmorency," which had been taken by the hospital staff from the brand name on the tool bag still clasped to his chest when the porters had carried him in. Two courtroom guards had to support him as he stood to hear the judge's sentence. Montmorency became prisoner 493 at the new prison, where the warden was fascinated by Doctor Farcett's continuing efforts to rebuild his body. The warden and the doctor took to meeting for dinner and an exchange of views about punishment and public health, agreeing on the need to attack crime by providing work, education, and better sanitation for the families whose ignorance and squalor bred common criminals.

Doctor Farcett became a familiar figure at the jail, and the warden gave him permission to take Montmorency, under guard, to meetings in town where eminent or aspiring physicians and scientists told of their own achievements and wanted to hear about Farcett's pioneering techniques.

It was at those gatherings, sitting almost naked under a blanket at the back of the rostrum, that Montmorency learned as much as anyone present. Though ignored by everyone until it was time for his scars to be exhibited before them, he heard of major advances in medicine, engineering, mathematics, and natural philosophy. A habitual thief, he continued to steal. With no pockets for his booty, he stole ideas and facts, committing to memory every detail of each lecture. He had no plans for putting the information to any use, but it interested him and gave him something to think about in the long hours of drudgery in the prison workshop or idleness in the infirmary after Doctor Farcett's operations.

As Montmorency lay there in pain on that dark, cold morning, he reflected on a long and, for him, rather eventful presentation by the chief engineer to the Metropolitan Board of Works. Suddenly, he had an idea. By the time Nurse Darnley was at his side with a battered tin mug, he had the makings of the scheme that would transform his life.

2. SIR JOSEPH BAZALGETTE

The lecture had been about London's new sewerage system. For almost twenty years the capital had been scarred by the filth and inconvenience of roadwork and construction sites. Gangs of laborers had shoveled tons of earth, and made and laid millions of bricks to produce eighty-three miles of underground tunnels through which the smelly and dangerous waste of the city could be taken away to be dumped nearer to the mouth of the Thames. Now the enterprise was complete, and Sir Joseph Bazalgette, the man who had planned and supervised the work, proudly described the achievement that had won him international recognition, and a knighthood from the Queen.

Taking the stage at the Scientific Society, Sir Joseph was a mixture of confidence and fear. He had a total command of his subject, but Montmorency could tell that he felt socially inferior to many of his audience, which included a couple of the more intelligent members of the House of Lords, as well as distinguished academics and a few visitors from abroad. Bazalgette was a short, neat man, with a thin nose and clever, dark eyes that seemed to be able to fix upon everyone in the room. His clothes were smart but fashionable: checked trousers and a plain jacket over a yellow waistcoat. His shirt collar was tied high at the neck with a silky cravat. A few strands of hair hopelessly tried to disguise the glistening baldness at the top of his head. Then suddenly, around his ears, his black locks grew rich and bushy, joining up via dainty sideburns with triangles of shiny, springy beard and a generous mustache. His chin was as bald as his head. Montmorency wondered why, when the rest of his face was so hairy, he bothered to shave that one little egg shape. Did he do it himself or did he have someone else to judge exactly where the razor should go? And how often did he need to shave it? There was no sign of shadow, even though it was six o'clock at night.

To get the audience on his side, Bazalgette opened his talk with a lighthearted explanation of his unusual name.

"French, originally, though my family has been here for three generations, and I'm proud to say that my father was an officer in the Royal Navy. But, of course, through my work I know all too well that human beings of all nationalities and classes have more similarities than differences — and that when it comes to their waste products, those of the nobility are just as noxious as those of the humblest peasant. It was for the good of all, great and small, that the Metropolitan Board of Works took upon itself the duty of disposing of that waste hygienically, endowing me with the honor and, if I may say so, the privilege of undertaking that task."

As Sir Joseph pointed out, everyone in the hall that night had reason to be thankful. Only a few years earlier that very building, for all its carved pillars and fine wood paneling, would have been a horrible place to spend an evening.

"As I made my way here this afternoon, I reflected on how conveniently located this great Scientific Society is. I came direct from the center of town and enjoyed my walk down towards the river. Children were playing in the streets. People were walking casually along the new Victoria Embankment, engaged in the harmless pleasure of taking the air. Yet many of you may remember how, not so long ago, a visit to this neighborhood was to be avoided. How even the chambers of Parliament itself were rank with the stink of raw sewage in the Thames. The truth is that, as this city grew to become the heart of a glorious empire, the old sluices and underground rivers that our forefathers relied upon to keep it clean proved totally inadequate. The new flushing toilets, so welcome in those lucky homes that owned them, completely overwhelmed those ancient drains and, across the capital, citizens were losing their lives to diseases born out of filth. And that filth tried to escape the city in the only way it could: straight into the river that flows by us here. I venture to suggest that had I come here twenty years ago to exhibit my original proposals, rather than to celebrate the completed scheme as I do now, my audience might have been rather smaller!"

The assembled scientists, politicians, and interested laymen tittered politely. Then they settled back on the curved leather benches that enclosed the stage in a horseshoe, and Sir Joseph relaxed a little, ready to deliver the body of his lecture.

"Earlier, I mentioned the Embankments. And I am proud of those grand boulevards alongside the river. Indeed, I am delighted to announce to you today that we contemplate their illumination with the new electric light within five years. But I urge you to turn your minds to what lies beneath. Not just to the underground trains that may have brought you here today. Not just to the gas pipes, which conduct to us the power to see so clearly in this hall. Not just to the water pipes that bring health and cleanliness along their path. Gentlemen, when you next find yourself strolling in the London streets, turn your eyes to the pavement, and look for the manholes that are the gateway to our new subterranean world. It is a world of giant tunnels, where thousands of gallons of water and, as one might say, 'more solid waste' are coursing beneath your feet, hour after hour, on their way to the sea."

Sir Joseph produced a huge map showing the layout of the sewers. It was beautifully drawn and hand colored, mounted on a heavy board. Two porters were always on duty at the Scientific Society, ready to hold up or pass around specimens provided by visiting speakers. Usually they had to cope with nothing heavier than a brain in a jar, plants, or perhaps a stuffed animal brought back from exotic parts by some intrepid traveler. This map, taller than Sir Joseph himself and almost as wide as the stage, was too much for them. They needed help, and Bazalgette motioned for Montmorency, who was sitting at the back of the stage waiting to be shown off in Doctor Farcett's talk, to come forward and assist them.

At the time, Montmorency was more embarrassed than interested. As usual, for the purposes of the doctor's demonstration, he was dressed in nothing but the skimpiest of underwear and, although he was now accustomed to being displayed as an object in this state, he felt like a fool standing there with his arms in the air, helping to balance the unwieldy chart. To make things worse, Sir Joseph banged on the map with a long stick as he traced the passage of the filthy liquid on its way around London. Every time he struck the board it wobbled precariously, and Montmorency and the porters wobbled with it. Once, as Sir Joseph showed the dramatic underground voyage of an imaginary turd from Buckingham Palace via the Houses of Parliament and along the new Embankment, he hit the map so hard that all three men lurched dangerously near to the edge of the platform. Montmorency felt his pants starting to descend. There were sniggers from the back of the hall and out of the corner of his eye he caught sight of Doctor Farcett with his head in his hands.

3. PLANNING

It was only much later, on that chilly morning in the prison hospital, that Montmorency realized how great a gift Sir Joseph Bazalgette had delivered. The map of the sewers, now imprinted on his mind because of his humiliation on the stage, could be the guide to his future career of crime. The tunnels were a new and secret route around London, serving, indeed, the richest areas, where the most profitable thieving could be done.

He lay there constructing a series of fantasy raids: seeing himself emerging from a hole in the ground, smashing, grabbing, and disappearing again as his victims and the flat-footed police ran around above his head frantically seeking the robber. He could almost feel the diamonds in his hand as he staged and restaged each crime. He wasn't stupid. He knew there would be difficulties. In fact, the more he thought about the plan, the more difficulties he foresaw. But Montmorency knew that, locked up in prison, he had time, and he resolved to dedicate the years until his release to solving those problems, and to devising the perfect method for getting as rich as the men who had giggled at him at the Scientific Society. This was going to be something far bigger than the petty thieving that had filled his life since childhood. But it needed to be worked out to the tiniest detail....

His dreams were interrupted by the sound of conversation outside the door. It wasn't the usual mumbled chat of the guards, but two cultured, excited voices.

"If you're going to make a habit of visiting this early, Robert, you might as well stay the night! Though the accommodation might not be up to your usual standard, and I've heard the porridge is a bit lumpy today!"

It was the prison warden on his early morning rounds. The other voice belonged to Doctor Farcett.

"I've had an idea about that scar on his back. The one where I cut through to get out the metal spike — you know, where the lung was pierced and I had that problem with the spleen."

Montmorency's whole body tightened at the memory of that early operation. He slid his arm behind his back and fingered the bulging scar that ran from his hip to his shoulder blade. He couldn't see it, but if it was anything like the ones on the rest of his body, it would be purple and shiny, with little dots along it marking the entry and exit points of every stitch.

"I was so much less experienced then. I've been awake all night thinking how I might have closed the wound differently, and I wouldn't mind a look at what's going on inside. Couldn't see a thing for the blood and bruising at the time. I'm just popping in to see if he's well enough for me to have another go. I'd like a crack at it, but I can't risk losing him before my big presentation in March."

"Well," said the warden, "drop in at my office if you've got time, anyway. And we re having dinner on Thursday, remember. Charles is bringing that Scotsman to tell us about his work on electricity."

"I'll be there. Now I'd better press on. I've got to get back to see a patient at nine."

Nurse Darnley had overheard the conversation, too, and was bustling around the room, straightening things up in preparation for the doctor's arrival. Her face reddened slightly as he entered, and Montmorency realized that it wasn't just a professional or even a motherly admiration that she felt for him.

Doctor Farcett was indeed a handsome man. His interest in the human body led him to treat his own with great respect, and he exercised regularly to keep it healthy. At Cambridge he had joined the college rowing club, and even now, well into his twenties, he would occasionally take part in races, so that although he was not a heavy man his chest was broad and his shoulders strong. His hair was a deep glossy brown, swept back from his forehead. He was clean. In fact, "clean" was the word Montmorency would have used first if he were asked to describe Robert Farcett. The doctor was forever washing his hands, demanding bowls of hot water and soap at all times. Nurse Darnley was boiling up the kettle for him now, unwrapping a new bar of the pungent carbolic soap that gave the infirmary its characteristic smell. Montmorency knew that, before he so much as pulled back the sheet, Farcett would be scrubbing away at every inch from his wrist to his fingertips, leaving his hands soft and white, like a lady's. His fingernails were short and shiny, filed into smooth curves with not even the slightest trace of dirt underneath. Sometimes Montmorency loathed those fingernails. For him, the clean hands brought pain. They had saved him, but they also showed him off in public like an animal in the zoo.

That morning, as Farcett prodded and poked at him, Montmorency tried to take his mind off his discomfort by continuing to make plans for his new life. He enjoyed picturing his daring raids, but he had a problem. How was he going to get rid of the things he stole? In the old days it had been simple. When he stole food, he ate it. The clothes, he wore. If there was anything he didn't want, he could usually find someone with whom to swap, or who might even give a little money in exchange. But in his new world, things would be different. He was dreaming of "society" burglaries, and you couldn't just turn up in a jeweler's shop looking like an ex-convict and claiming that the necklace you wanted to sell was a family heirloom. He would need a new class of contacts and, for the moment, the only place he could look for them was in the prison itself. But what better pool of information could there be? Between them, the thieves, fraudsters, and degenerates with whom he shared his days should have all the information he needed to carry out his new enterprise. They weren't all masters of their art — after all, they'd all been caught — but some of them were very experienced and it would be a shame to let their talents go to waste.

4. PRISON LIFE

To Montmorency's great relief, Doctor Farcett decided, for the time being, not to risk reopening the long scar down his back. So, when his thigh had healed, he was sent back to the cell he shared with two other men in the main prison block. It had been designed for one prisoner. Indeed, the authorities had originally intended that convicts should be kept apart at all times, so that they could not corrupt one another further, but crime was rising faster than new prisons could be built, and soon there were two, and then three, to a cell.

Sometimes Montmorency was glad of the company. More often he was repulsed by the stench from the bucket the three of them shared as a lavatory, which they were allowed to empty only once a day, in a long, stinking procession to the washhouse. These days, as he slopped its contents down the sluice, he imagined it making its way through pipes and streams to Bazalgette's underground world, where it would mix with the waste from the comfortable homes of his future victims in the city.

His two companions were both older than him, and more used to prison life. Barney Watts, a vicious thug who trusted no one, was one of a large family who had graduated from the streets of Clapham to prison with the same inevitability that had taken Robert Farcett from prep school through university. Some of Watts's brothers had died on the gallows, having aimed too high and stolen from people of influence. His stories of their last hours were a constant reminder to Montmorency of the need to take care in his new life. The prizes might be great, but the cost of getting caught would be greater still.

Frank Holliday, his other cell mate, was a small-time pickpocket with one leg and no teeth. Unlike Watts, he had no major crimes to his name, only a series of convictions resulting from bungled thefts committed without planning or skill. But he did boast of an uncle transported to Australia for organizing prizefights in the street. The three convicts would make up stories about what might have happened to that uncle. On some nights, they imagined him lost on the long sea voyage. On others, he was eaten by cannibals or kangaroos. Sometimes they let him make a fortune as a sheep farmer and imagined him sneaking back to England to collect his nephew for a new life of prosperity in the sun.

Frank's other claim to fame was his ability to imitate people. After only a few moments' acquaintance he could capture the essence of an inmate or a guard. Best of all, he could make faces. Not just the occasional grimace directed at the back of a hated guard, but elaborate manglings of his nose, lips, and eyeballs that transformed his face into a horrific mask. With his eyes pointing in two directions, widened as if they were about to pop, his lips twisted, and his nose sucked in, he could turn the stomach of the most hardened criminal. Throughout the prison, even people who had never spoken to him knew him as "Freakshow Frank," who could entertain and revolt the whole dinner line, as long as no guards were watching. Freakshow reveled in the celebrity his talent gave him among the other inmates, and courted attention at all times. Barney Watts was more of a natural loner, skulking in corners, and turning away even the most well-meant glance of greeting with a brisk, "Had your look?"

Many times, Montmorency was tempted to tell Freakshow and Barney about his plan, but he instinctively felt it would be better to keep quiet. Instead, he would occasionally turn their late-night conversations to the subject of thieving, and how they would get rid of particularly expensive goods. But they were of little help, sometimes coming up with the names of crooked dealers, but then forgetting where they lived or remembering that they were in prison or even dead. Freakshow in particular seemed seduced by the idea of rich pickings, but was no use when it came to ideas for disposing of them. Occasionally, Montmorency tried to talk to other prisoners in the workshop or while lining up for food, but most of them turned against him in disgust. It was known that Montmorency, prisoner 493, was regularly taken away from the jail in a carriage and that he spent long periods in the imagined comfort of the infirmary. They hated him for it. Some of them looked at him with such loathing that he feared for his safety.

He was lining up to empty his bucket one morning when two guards clanked up the metal staircase from the floor below.

"Get a move on, scum," barked the taller of the two, pushing past along the side of the line, forcing the prisoners against one another. Montmorency's bucket was very full — Barney Watts had been sick all night — and some of the contents slopped over the edge, onto the man in front. It was 596, doing time for a drunken rampage at Paddington Station, but rumored to have been responsible for several knifings, unreported to the police by his terrified victims. As Montmorency struggled to stutter an apology, 596 turned and grabbed him, twisting the top of his shirt into his neck so hard that Montmorency could barely breathe. Their two buckets dropped noisily onto the cast-iron mesh of the floor, the mixture inside pouring out and dripping through to the other levels.

"I'll kill you for that," spat out 596, his cracked, stinking teeth only inches away from Montmorency's face, which was turning red and then blue. Montmorency tried to speak but all that came out was a strangled squeal. His bulging eyes appealed to the guards for help, but they just stood and watched the assault, intervening only when he was on the point of passing out, and then taking 596's side, twisting Montmorency's arm high up behind his back as they kicked and pummeled him against the wall, leaving him gasping in a heap.

"Get up and clean up this mess," snarled the tall guard, kicking him again when he failed to jump to the command. "What's the matter — were you expecting us to send you to the hospital?"

The other convicts laughed at this remark and, though they were silenced with a quick "Shut up" and the slap of a billy club across the face of the nearest man, from then on the prisoners behaved as if they had official permission to taunt Montmorency whenever they pleased. When he held out his bowl for porridge, the man on kitchen duty would suddenly find that the ladle was only half full. The tea in his mug might contain an extra floating gob of white phlegm. In the workshop, hammers slipped and caught his thumb. In the laundry, boiling water "accidentally" splashed his foot. A door might close on his arm. He was tripped in the exercise yard. The guards saw nothing or chose not to. Barney Watts went out of his way to be unkind when other prisoners were around, and even Freakshow took care not to appear friendly outside the whispering intimacy of the cell. They were both afraid that their forced association with 493 might get them into trouble with the hard men, too.

5. MEASURING UP

"493!" barked the guard, rapping on the door with his huge bunch of keys. It was Marston, the menacing custodian from the infirmary. "You've got one of your little outings tonight. Here's the doctor come to see you again." He spat out the word "doctor" with as much disdain as he used for "493," even though he added, "Get up and show a bit of respect."

Freakshow and Barney moved to one corner of the cell, pretending to take no notice, but watching intently as the door clanked open and Marston's vast form made way for the trim young man to enter.

Doctor Farcett fumbled with his bag. He knew that the guards regarded his visits to the prison with suspicion, and that they saw Montmorency's frequent stays in the hospital wing and occasional trips to the lecture theater as treats. He suspected that Montmorency suffered at their hands and that the other prisoners were jealous, too. He had seen the new bruises. But he had said nothing. Instead, he made a point of being offhand with his patient whenever he was in the company of the prison guards — indeed, he usually spoke to Montmorency entirely through them. If asked, he would probably have had difficulty remembering his name. "493" tripped off the tongue more freely, and was certainly easier to write in notes and say to an audience than the ridiculous Frenchified surname "Montmorency" that his patient had acquired along the way.

Montmorency was amused to see Farcett, who was usually relaxed with the warden and so confident when demonstrating his handiwork to the intellectuals at the Scientific Society, so ill at ease with the lugubrious guard.

"I have to check some measurements before tonight's lecture. Can you get him to stand with his arms outstretched?"

The doctor got out a measuring tape and motioned to the guard to take one end. Marston coughed, and affected not to notice the request, so Doctor Farcett stretched across Montmorency himself, pencil in mouth, stopping after each measurement to note it down in a small black book. Montmorency noticed then, for the first time, the almost exact match between himself and the surgeon. It was as if a more prosperous version of himself were reflected in a mirror, doing some strange dance, arm to arm, leg to leg. Montmorency was thinner and weaker, of course, after all his operations.

As if he had realized this at the same moment, Farcett muttered, as much to himself as to Marston, "Poor muscle tone in the upper body ... Must see the warden about some exercise or hard labor."

Marston's eyes brightened at the last two words and, as he shackled himself to Montmorency for the trip to town, he was even rougher than usual. "We'll see how our favorite patient likes hard work then, won't we, 493?" he sneered, snapping the handcuffs tight.

Freakshow made a sympathetic face, while Watts couldn't stop a malevolent sneer that convinced Montmorency he'd been wise not to let slip of his secrets in their late night chats.

Montmorency said nothing. He'd realized as the doctor spoke that heavy labor was just what he needed. If he was to survive life in the sewers, he would have to regain the fitness he'd had before his fall — the physique that had made him the best sportsman on his street and ensured that until the night of his accident he had never once been caught by the police.

6. *F*ARCETT'S
HOUSE

The dark carriage was waiting in the gap between the inner and outer walls of the prison. It had been adapted from an ordinary London cab, but the window was blocked out to stop inquisitive bystanders from looking in, and the only view from inside was through little slits where the roof met the sides. Marston, who disapproved of the warden letting a prisoner travel around London in such a way, was even more disdainful when Farcett asked the driver to take a detour to his home.

"I have to collect some illustrations of his original wounds," he explained to the guard. Marston felt like saying that he didn't care why he was stopping off. It was most irregular and shouldn't be allowed. But he confined himself to a shrug and a grunt, which left the doctor feeling just as uneasy as if Marston had spelled out his views in full.

By the time they reached Holland Park, Farcett was so uncomfortable that he jumped from the van without closing the door properly.

"I'll just nip in the back — Wednesday is the maid's afternoon off."

Before Marston had reached across him to shut the door, Montmorency caught a glimpse of the doctor's house. It was larger than he had expected, surrounded by a substantial garden and a high brick wall, but the back gate was unlocked. In his haste, Farcett left that open, too, and could be seen hurrying across the lawn, up three wide, curved steps to some French windows. Again, there was no sign of a key being needed as the doctor disappeared inside.

Montmorency's criminal instincts were alert in a second. What a pity he was chained to the guard. But the information was filed away in his memory anyway, alongside the developing plan for his return to London crime.

At the Scientific Society that night, Montmorency found himself drawing up a potential list of victims as Doctor Farcett invited several colleagues to examine the jagged scar on his patient's back and to suggest how it might be modified. Should he reenter the wound along the same line, cutting out the old lumpy scar tissue, or perform an incision at a new site? Under the arm perhaps? Or along the belly? As a succession of hands slid along his skin, Montmorency could feel heavy gold rings, smell expensive hair oil, catch glimpses of pocket watches and tie pins. The thick wool of substantial jackets brushed his naked body, warm and rough against his goose pimples.

The only hint of kindness came from Professor Humbley. He was a philosopher, who had just given a lecture on logical reasoning, which Montmorency had found more entertaining than he'd expected. Professor Humbley was clearly a man rather embarrassed by his own body, let alone someone else's, and when Doctor Farcett encouraged him to join the others in their examination, he did so with reluctance, more out of politeness than enthusiasm. After the briefest of strokes along Montmorency's back, with a hand as soft as a child's, he seemed to mutter a brief, Thank you.

The next man was less gentle, pushing down on the livid scars to see if the color drained away under pressure, and manipulating Montmorency's arm like the handle on a pump to see how the shoulder joint was recovering from being wrenched apart in the fall. His breath smelled of fine wine and a good dinner. As he stepped from the stage, he wiped his fingers on a silk handkerchief, as if contaminated by touching Montmorency's body. It was a gesture of arrogant superiority that Montmorency would not forget. He'd get that handkerchief, and more, from its owner one day.

7. THE WALL

Marston made sure that Montmorency was put on hard labor immediately. There was plenty to do. Although the prison was new, it was already being extended and, to keep costs down, the work was done by the inmates themselves, using stone from a local quarry and making bricks from the thick London clay beneath their feet. Marston was disappointed at Montmorency's willingness for the task. Doctor Farcett was impressed by the improvement in his physical strength, and Montmorency used his time breaking stones and shoveling cement to perfect his plans.

The more Montmorency mixed with Doctor Farcett and observed the members of the Scientific Society, the more convinced he was that he would never return to his old place at the bottom end of London's lowlife. He knew what he was aiming at and was convinced that with the sewer plan he had found the ideal method for making his fortune, but — as Professor Humbley might have said — there was "an obvious logical error in the proposal." It was this:

Sewage stinks, but rich people, on the whole, don't. The wealthy lifestyle Montmorency wanted would require a constant supply of funds, so he would have to keep thieving, but since he couldn't do that in a top hat and tails, he'd have to live in an area where someone who dressed and behaved like a sewer worker would not attract attention. That would be all very well in the early days when he was amassing his first funds, but how would he ever be able to enjoy his wealth without arousing suspicions?

One day, carrying a heavy trough of bricks in the hope of building up his shoulders, he came up with what he thought was the answer. Or rather, Freakshow Frank gave it to him.

Freakshow had been given the job of building one of the main supporting walls of the new cell block. His early efforts at bricklaying had been wobbly and uneven, but the sheer repetition involved in the job had brought with it a certain skill and, though he would never have admitted it, he had begun to take pride in his work.

"Bring us some more bricks over here, 493," he shouted to Montmorency, who was loading up his trough. "And keep them coming. I bet you I can get this finished by dinnertime."

Barney Watts looked on suspiciously, angry with his cell mate for pushing the pace of the work, but Montmorency piled on some extra bricks and made his way across the yard. By the time he had loaded up again, Freakshow was calling for more.

"Get a move on there — keep the pace up, you weed."

"493, wee-wee-dee," muttered Watts under his breath — meaning it as a private joke, but finding it picked up by the men around him and converted into a mass chant. "493, wee-wee-dee ..."

To everyone's amazement, Montmorency didn't react with anger, but with increased pace, matching his movements to the rhythm of the men. The guard, who at first was going to intervene, was so surprised that he pulled back and watched, his billy club tapping the beat against his leg.

Soon everyone except Freakshow and Montmorency was at a standstill, watching as 493 delivered endless supplies to the manic bricklayer, who buttered each brick as if he were icing a cake, and then fixed it in place with delicacy and speed. They kept going until the wall was higher than Freakshow's ladder. Then Montmorency slumped forward, his hands on his knees, to get his breath back.

There was a hint of applause before the guard remembered his job and angrily urged the rest of the men back to their duties. Freakshow hopped and swung his one-legged way down the ladder, and put his hand on Montmorency's shoulder for balance.

"We were a great team there."

"Silence!" shouted the guard.

But it was enough. Montmorency knew now what he needed to make his plan work.

He would have to get an accomplice.

8. MONTMORENCY
AND SCARPER

So Montmorency's plan took a new turn. He would start the sewer business himself, and then let someone else in to do the dirty work while he enjoyed the life of a dandy in town.

He spent hours drawing up deals in his head, working out how big a percentage the underground man would get, and he ran through some possible candidates for the job. Sadly, Freakshow was out of the question because of his missing leg and Barney Watts's sour suspiciousness ruled him out of any form of team-work. But back home there was Mickey Grady, his old friend from Sunday school, who was very strong and known throughout the neighborhood for stealing a leg of pork one Christmas and running fast enough to get it into the oven before the butcher could catch up with him. And what about Nobby North, reputed to be double jointed, who could bend himself into all sorts of positions? (Bound to be an advantage going up and down drains, surely?) Then there was "Bonkers" Harry Baines, the foolhardy but loyal old crook who had recruited Montmorency for the factory job that had so nearly cost him his life. Even here in prison now, there must be men who would be out around the same time as

Montmorency, looking for work. Perhaps the promise of riches would help them overcome their distaste for him.

The next day, Sunday, Montmorency continued to talent-spot. As the prisoners formed a line, silent and sullen on their way to the weekly religious service, he sized them up. Many didn't seem fit enough for the underground life. Some looked at him with such contempt for his supposed privileges that he knew there was no point in approaching them. Others he placed on his mental list to speak to later, if the guards felt like allowing the weekly period of exercise and association that the warden thought had been introduced months ago.

He could do nothing now, for the prison chapel was cunningly constructed with wooden partitions along the pews so that each man sat in a tiny cubicle of his own, making it impossible for the prisoners to talk to one another. Coincidentally, the chapel was the same shape and size as the Scientific Society's lecture theater, with the semicircular rows of seats steeply raked and looking down on to the altar and the little apron of "stage" in front of it. But the atmosphere was completely different. There was none of the conviviality of Doctor Farcett's favorite audience. The chaplain spoke as if to a crowd, and during the hymn and the Lord's Prayer when the prisoners joined in the singing and chanting, it was clear that plenty of men were present, but they couldn't communicate with one another at all.

Strangely, Montmorency found himself communicating instead with Professor Humbley. Not the man himself, but a jovial apparition — complete with heaving shoulders, sweaty forehead, and toothy giggle — conjured up in Montmorency's memory as the chaplain intoned, "Humbly we beseech thee ..."

The jolly logician had popped into Montmorency's thoughts to point out another devastating flaw in his plan.

"Think about it, old boy. All your prospective accomplices are criminals!"

Professor Humbley was right. Montmorency was proposing to reveal his ingenious method of getting around London, and would then expect them either to turn down the job, keep the secret, and let him get on with it, or do the stealing for him and keep their promise to pass him the best part of the proceeds. But why should they? Would he, in the same circumstances?

The phantom professor danced before him, chortling, "Fat chance, old boy, fat chance."

Montmorency sat through the sermon in despair. His plan was in ruins. He couldn't work with an accomplice. He couldn't enjoy being rich without one. He couldn't live the life of a sewer rat and the life of a gentleman at the same time.

Or could he?

By the time the chaplain was uttering the blessing, and dispatching his flock back to their cells, Montmorency had the answer: He would become his own accomplice. His old self would become the servant of his new self. One would live in squalor, the other in style.

"Spot on," giggled the fat old philosopher. "Marvelous! I do congratulate you on the essential economy and simplicity of your proposal."

The gloom lifted. As the men filed out of the chapel, Montmorency was already making plans again. He was back where he was happiest: in his own head, running over the intricate details of his new life. For a start, what should he call himself (or rather, himselves)?

He thought "Montmorency" was a stylish upper-class-sounding name. He'd rather taken to it since the accident that had brought it his way, and had never revealed his true identity to anyone since. Yes, he would keep "Montmorency" for the life of luxury.

His other self— scurrying, skulking, thieving, and paddling around in sewage — needed a more appropriate label. But not his old name. His old voice — all his old mannerisms and attitudes, yes — but no link with his past identity. After all, the whole plan was designed to cut him loose from that world.

493 contemplated several options as he lay awake that night: names of old playmates, enemies, dogs; names taken from pub signs, street names, nicknames. In the end, as he was falling asleep and his recurring dream about the rooftop chase started up, he hit on it. Back at the factory where he'd had his near-fatal fall, Bonkers Baines had shouted one word when he heard the policeman's whistle: "SCARPER!"

9. RELEASE

Montmorency had been so dazed at the time of his trial that he hadn't taken in the full details of his sentence. The other prisoners counted the days. Freakshow's release was imminent, and Watts knew he had years to go. Montmorency reckoned that more than three years had passed since his own arrest and, at times, he wondered if he was to be held for as long as Robert Farcett wanted to play with him. But he continued preparing for life after prison.

Lately, he had been working on his plan to operate in disguise, asking Freakshow to teach him the tricks of the impersonator's trade. Freakshow had shown him how to observe the way people walked, looking for the characteristic habitual gesture or tic that made each person an individual. He pointed out how the way you hold your mouth affects the way you talk: how the cockney accent of most of the prisoners was formed almost completely at the front of the mouth; how Doctor Farcett and the warden produced their rounder sounds by keeping their lips and tongues more mobile and breathing lower in the chest; and how an aristocratic do-gooder who had toured the prison and made a speech to the inmates exhorting them to reform had pinched his vowel sounds behind his teeth and hardly used his facial muscles at all — "Ind seuw, when you ere bick with your fiamilies, resooelve to stay orf the parth of vice, and stick to the nirrow way."

One morning they were imitating the prison guards, listening for the rhythms of their steps and guessing who was passing by on the corridor outside. Barney Watts slouched on his bunk, too bitter to join in the theatricals (even though none of his hard friends could have seen him), but guessing the identities of the characters as each charade was acted out. Montmorency was doing a passable takeoff of one of the rougher guards who shuffled and coughed as he walked, when the footsteps outside the cell stopped and a key turned in the lock.

"493," said the voice that went with the walk. "You're wanted in the warden's office."

Montmorency had never been in that room before. Though it was sparsely furnished and, like the cells, had only a small high window, it seemed luxurious compared with the rest of the building. Two of the walls were covered with well-stocked bookshelves. The others were decorated with paintings of rural scenes, a framed copy of the prison rules, and a portrait of the Queen in her younger days. There was a rug on the floor, with the warden's broad desk sitting in the middle of it. Its leather top was covered with neat piles of papers, an elaborate inkwell in the shape of a fish, and a selection of books, one of which, he noted, was Professor Humbley's work on the philosophical background to the French Revolution.

The warden sat behind the desk in a wide wooden chair with a high back, its curved arms upholstered in the same green leather as the desk. As he reached across for documents, it swiveled with the movement of his body. When he spoke, he could rock back and forth as he made a point. When he stood up, the chair rolled back on castors to make way for him. It was clear that the warden loved his chair. It was his private little toy, a bit of fun in his drab surroundings. Montmorency wanted that chair. He fancied the inkwell, too, but could see that it was screwed to the desk to prevent theft or its use as a missile by an angry inmate.

"Well, 493," said the warden, "the time has come for you to leave us."

At first Montmorency wondered if he was being transferred to another prison, but then the warden continued, "You have completed your sentence, and it is time for you to return to the world outside. I have been most interested in your progress here and am pleased to see that your recovery from your injuries is complete."

Here, the guard let out a grunting cough, which eloquently expressed his contempt for the "soft" treatment the warden had allowed 493, with all his doctoring and trips to town. Once again, Montmorency remarked to himself how effectively the guards could discomfort their superiors with unvoiced disdain.

The warden cut short his speech. "But it is time for you to go. Your possessions will be returned to you downstairs. You have been given the chance of life, 493. I hope you will take the opportunity to make that life one of industry and law-abiding behavior." He pushed back his chair and swiveled around to open a drawer at the side. "I must also give you this."

It was a bulky envelope, sealed, but apparently containing several sheets of paper and some coins.

"You are fortunate that someone—" he eyed the inquisitive guard — "who must remain nameless here, has seen fit to help you on your way. Now leave. I do not wish to have you back in my care again."

For a moment, it seemed to Montmorency that the warden was going to offer a handshake, but once more the guard grunted, and the warden drew back, averting his eyes as 493 was hustled from the room.

Montmorency never got to see the contents of the envelope. The guard took it from him before they reached the stairs. He wondered what it had been. Perhaps a handout and a tract from some religious body? Or even — though it didn't seem very likely — something from Freakshow's Australian uncle? Anyway, the guard took it, and Montmorency would be leaving prison as he had entered it — with nothing.

And so, suddenly, he wasn't prisoner 493 anymore. Downstairs, they gave him civilian clothes, the same ones he'd worn to his trial. After his accident, a nurse at the hospital had found them somewhere, perhaps on an unfortunate corpse. It didn't do to think too much about where they'd come from. His own clothes had been ripped and bloodstained in the fall, or torn from him as Farcett struggled, against the advice of everyone around him, to save Montmorency's life. Even in court the replacements hadn't fit. Now, after more than three years in prison, half of it spent in muscle-building labor, they were comically small. The jacket stretched across his shoulders, pulling up the sleeves well clear of his wrists. The trousers strained to cover his calves. Montmorency didn't mind — it showed how strong and fit he had become, ready for the task ahead. And anyway, if he hadn't lost his old skills, it wouldn't be long before he got something better.

The prison had been built among fields, on the edge of a large common. Diagonally opposite, several hundred yards away, there was a small line of shops. Montmorency had caught tiny glimpses of the local area from the van on his trips into town with Doctor Farcett, but he knew nothing of this district on the edge of London and, despite all the hours spent nurturing his Grand Plan, he was suddenly uncertain of what to do when the prison doors thundered shut behind him, and the routines of his life inside were taken away. He made for the shops, starting to cross the grass that, at first, was thrillingly fresh and soft after years of walking only on stone, but soon gave way to a muddy bog, sucking his boots into its early morning squelch. The solid pathway back around the side of the high prison wall looked more inviting, and he joined it even though he was unsure where it led.

A large, weary figure shuffled along a few yards ahead of him, curiously familiar as it dragged one foot lazily after the other, stopping occasionally to raise a bottle to its mouth. As the man turned the corner, out of sight, Montmorency realized who it was. Marston, the night guard from the prison hospital, had finished his shift and was on his way home.

Montmorency tried to catch up, carefully staying well enough behind to avoid being seen. The lane came to an end at a terrace of tiny new houses, identical except for their front yards. Some had regimented borders of violently orange marigolds; others were monuments to hours of industrious digging, with square blocks of the same heavy black earth he had trudged into on the common. Here and there were signs of successful cultivation, lines of lettuce, onions, or green beans trailing up canes. One plot was a tangle of disorganized color where a passing mania for gardening had been overindulged, and the plants left to fight it out among themselves. Another was simply a neatly cut oblong of grass. Next door, at the end of the row, there was a heartless dump of old metal, rusty tools, nettles, and weeds. The houses were all built from the same gray bricks he had spent so much time hauling around the prison yard, so they matched the huge jail whose mighty defenses cut out all light from their humble backyards. They looked like a line of tiny lifeboats nestling up alongside a huge warship. They were the prison guards' homes.

Montmorency watched Marston's progress. It was no surprise to see him make for that final ramshackle yard, pausing only to brush away the attentions of a large ugly dog and to feel the graying clothes that must have been hanging all night on the sagging washing line. No doubt they were still wet. He didn't take them down, but slouched into the house, slamming the door behind him. Marston, who had seemed so fearsome and powerful at his workplace, was transformed into a lumbering hopeless figure by real life.

But Montmorency was in no mood to pity him. He knew an opportunity when he saw it, and slipped behind an unkempt hedge towards the washing. He grabbed a damp shirt and, wrapping it around his shoulders to dry as he walked, set off back down the lane towards the road to town.

10. $\mathcal{I}$NTO LONDON

By the time he reached Westminster he was Scarper, in possession of a small purse of coins — thanks to Freakshow's lessons in pickpocketing — and fully dressed in a new set of clothes stolen one by one as he took his chances along the way. The washing line crop had been particularly abundant that morning, but he was most pleased by the boots, which he'd first spotted on a nightwatchman at a cheese warehouse in Chelsea. He had been contemplating breaking in to get some food, but when the day shift arrived and the man left, Scarper had decided to follow him home instead.

He'd heard the wife's nagging before the front door was even shut.

"I'm not having those filthy boots in here. Two hours I spent scrubbing that floor, and you just walk in as if you own the place."

"I do own the place.'"

"Oh, very funny. Well, if you own the bloody place, you can bloody well clean it and bloody well feed your own bloody baby that's kept me up all night — all on my own without you!"

"I was working. Where do you think the money comes from around here?"

"You call that working? You just sit in that hut drinking. I'll show you work. You look at the state of this. Worn to pieces!"

Scarper ducked as the heavy wooden scrub brush flew out into the street.

"And now you come in in your muddy boots. Well, you can muddy well take them off now!"

"Right then, I will.'"

And Scarper had caught them as they flew out, too. A minute later, when he'd sneaked around the corner to try them on, he heard the baby launching into a hearty wail.

Two lessons learned. Work and marriage were not for him.

Now Scarper was making for the Houses of Parliament, and more particularly for the risqué statue of Queen Boadicea and her bare-breasted daughters that stood opposite Big Ben, at the end of the bridge. It crowned Bazalgette's new embankment, the long riverside road under which a giant sewer made its way to the east. Here, there should be a manhole, a way into a new world of riches. As visitors to London raised their eyes to admire the Parliament building and the Abbey, and workers stared blankly ahead on the way to their jobs, Scarper concentrated on the pavement, looking for the doorway to his dreams.

There it was. Black, round, made of heavy metal, but cast in a decorative mold with a pattern and the proud insignia of the Metropolitan Board of Works. Sunk in to one side was a short bar. A handle for lifting it, perhaps? Scarper was desperate to have a try. He bent down, as if to tie his shoelace.

"Hey, watch out there!" cried a man, stumbling over him in his hurry to cross the bridge.

"Sorry, sir," said Scarper, fingering his stolen cap in a gesture of respect and apology.

He stayed down, gingerly slipping his fingers under the bar, hoping that with a quick pull he could lift the lid. People darted around him. One woman's coat brushed against him, knocking off his hat. He pulled. The huge black disk wouldn't budge. He looked up and saw a child gazing at him curiously. He tried an imitation of one of Freakshow's grimaces and, with a cry, the little boy hid his face in his mother's skirts.

Two more lessons learned. He would need some kind of lever to raise the manhole covers and, day or night, this was not the place to begin his adventures. There were too many people and too many of them were policemen. He needed somewhere more private, somewhere nearer to lodgings he could afford.

Following the line of the sewer map he remembered so well from Bazalgette's talk, he went from manhole to manhole, and found the perfect one in the maze of theaters, houses, markets, and churches in Covent Garden to the north of the Strand.

He found a room, too. He turned down a side street near the flower market and saw the word "Vakensees" chalked on the blackened wall of a narrow house. He thought it must be somebody's name until he noticed the faint mark of the word "No" scrubbed out in front of it.

A barefoot girl in her early teens was sitting on the doorstep. She was wearing a tattered petticoat, and her long hair hung down in a nest of tangles around her shoulders. She looked tired as she rubbed a filthy shoe with an even filthier rag. She didn't look up.

"Looking for a room?"

"Depends how much."

Now she raised her head, as if to estimate how much Scarper was worth.

"It's cheap. Lots of stairs, see."

"Can I have a look?"

"Up here."

He followed the girl up a narrow staircase, past a series of numbered doors to number eight on the top landing. She showed him a small, airless, and not entirely clean room with a bed, a table, and one rickety chair.

"You'll have to see my mum about the rent. She'll say no visitors, no pets, and no wet laundry indoors, and leave the facilities as you would expect to find them. She'll say you pay now in advance and every week on a Friday or you're out and she means out 'cos her brother works at the vegetable market and he can lift weights much heavier than you, and she won't wait for no excuses. She don't do food, and she won't have you doing no cooking in here. You work in the market?"

He was debating whether to lie and say he did work there when a panting noise and series of heaving thumps came from the staircase.

"Ooh, these knees are something shocking. I hope you're going to take the room now you've dragged me up here."

A larger, older version of the girl pulled herself up the stairs. She was wearing an old-fashioned yellow dress, probably someone else's castoff, as it was far too small across the chest, and rather too long at the bottom. The lace trim on the neckline and sleeves was graying, and coming apart in places. She wiped her nose on her arm as she leaned on the banister to get her breath back at the top.

"Who've you got here then, Vi?" she said, keeping her eyes, firmly on Scarper.

"He works in the market."

Scarper had no time to deny it before the woman chimed in, "Well, my brother works at the vegetable market, and he can lift weights heavier than you, so don't think you can be late with the rent. I won't wait for no excuses. Pay now in advance and then regular every Friday. No visitors, no pets, and no wet washing indoors, and leave the facilities as you would expect to find them. I don't do food, and I won't have you doing no cooking in here."

Scarper and Vi exchanged a conspiratorial glance. She had mimicked her mother to a tee.

"Name?"

"Scar—"

"Scar by name and scar by nature, I see!" She laughed, looking at his arm.

He rolled down his shirtsleeve to cover the wound, and handed over half his cash.

"My name's Evans," said the woman, "and this is Vi. She's a good girl. Good Evans we call her, and we want it to stay that way, don't we, Vi? And I'm warning you, my brother can take care of anything. We'll leave you to get settled in."

Scarper slumped onto the bed, exhausted by the mixture of threats and goodwill the Evans women had thrown at him. The dingy little room would have to do for now. He investigated "the facilities:" a stinking hole in a shed outside that lacked any apparent link with Sir Joseph Bazalgette's world of drains, and a metal sink with a dripping tap. Still, it was better than prison, and he looked forward to sleeping without a bucket of excrement at his side. But if he was to sustain even this meager lifestyle, he would need to get to work straightaway. He would have to make his first trip into the sewers that night. As he left the house, Mrs. Evans gave him a wink and a wave from the front room where she was sitting at the window, having her hair crimped by Vi with a huge pair of curling tongs. Vi herself was dressed now, in a mauve outfit and with an alarming amount of make-up on her face. Closing the front door behind him, he saw that a proud "No" had been reinstated before the "Vakensees" sign. It could almost be home.

Before he could venture underground, there was some more mundane thieving to do — he needed a lever to open the manhole. In his prison fantasies, he had imagined lifting these lids with a flick of the wrist. It was clear now that something else was called for, but what? It wasn't as if there were shops on every street corner selling sewer equipment for the man-about-town. In any case, he didn't want to pay for what was likely to be a fairly pricey item. All afternoon he scoured the market, the backs of warehouses, dumps, and trash cans for something that would do. No luck. The best thing he found was a strong piece of wood from the side of a packing crate. It simply shattered when he tried it. The metal lid was too heavy to lift. All those years of planning and it looked as if he would be defeated right at the start, as if he couldn't get the top off a boiled egg because he didn't have a spoon.

He was tired. He was hungry. He collapsed, dejected, into a pub and ordered a drink and a pie from a bored woman who smelled as if the great advances in London hygiene had completely passed her by. He ate slowly, glad to have a chance to take his own time over his food, but wondering whether he wouldn't be better off back in prison, still dreaming, still capable of hope.

Then he noticed the filthy barmaid jabbing at the sluggish fire with a long, sturdy poker. It was strong. It was metal. He had to have it. Ten minutes later, after the girl had waddled off to pay reluctant attention to another customer, Scarper was limping up the street with the poker down one leg of his trousers. He could be pretty sure that the barmaid wouldn't notice its absence for a while. She probably would notice that he hadn't paid for his lunch, though. But he wouldn't be going there again.

11. FIRST TRY

As soon as the street by his lodgings was clear, Scarper tried levering open the manhole cover. That was hard enough, but maneuvering it back over the hole as he descended into the dark shaft was the real test of his strength. Inside, the layout was just as Bazalgette had described, with a narrow metal ladder attached to the wall leading down to the foul river at the bottom. But Bazalgette hadn't mentioned that the ladder would be slimy, and Scarper struggled to hang on. He hadn't mentioned the dark, either. It was obvious, of course, now that Scarper was in the hole, but all the illustrations displayed at the Scientific Society had been in bright watercolors, and he hadn't thought to bring a light with him. Above all, Bazalgette hadn't mentioned the smell. It was a savage, suffocating stench that had Scarper fighting back his vomit. He had assumed that the acrid urine-scented air of the prison would have inured him against such a shock to his senses. He had been wrong, but he had gotten used to that smell, and he would get used to this. But not now. Not without a lamp and a proper plan of what he would do once he was down the ladder. Now he would go back up.

He slowly pressed against the underside of the lid. To his relief, it lifted, letting in some light, but to his alarm it let in an unwelcome sound as well. Two women were leaning against a wall, not ten feet away, chatting. He couldn't see them, but one set of throaty giggles sounded very like his new landlady. For what seemed like hours, Scarper stood, wedged against the underground ladder, the manhole lid held open just a crack, taking in endless details of the women's lives. He learned more than he would ever have wanted to know about their health, their living, and late husbands' shortcomings and those of someone else, called Tommy, whom they both seemed to know a great deal better than they should have. He was despairing of them ever leaving when one interrupted the other with, "Do you smell a smell?"

He jumped with the fear of being discovered, and lowered the cover an inch or two.

"Well, it's not mine, I haven't done nothing."

"Better be going anyhow, he'll be wanting his tea."

And, with a few false starts as they caught up on plans for a wedding and a rumor about a fight, they eventually made their way in opposite directions down the street, out of earshot and out of sight.

Scarper's relieved ascent from the hole wasn't quite as easy as he'd hoped. He moved the lid away using his head and shoulders, but then realized that hiding a long metal stick down your trouser leg was a mistake if you were trying to climb a ladder. Knees have to bend. In the end, the poker slipped away into the water below. He cursed aloud, only to find his words echoing around him with a mighty boom. He registered the need to keep quiet underground and added a stubby metal hook to his mental list of desirable equipment.

He had learned a lot, and he hadn't even reached the bottom of the ladder yet. But he was determined to try again the next night, and this time he would get it right.

12. THE FIRST JOB

Setting off on that mission, Scarper had a far better set of tools. He'd had the brain wave of going to the docks for what he needed and had soon noticed the short, heavy hooks used for maneuvering and opening crates. It wasn't long before someone put one down for a second, only to find it gone when he reached out for it again. The river was the place to find waterproof lanterns, too, and all sorts of twine and small bits of equipment somehow found their way into Scarper's pocket. At Billingsgate, brimming boxes of fish were being unloaded, and a fat, angry man with a streaming nose was writing up prices on a blackboard. He was angrier still when, after a sneeze that covered some of the cod prematurely in tartar sauce, he couldn't find his chalk.

That evening, a fine drizzle had emptied the street outside Scarper's rooms. This time he was down the shaft more elegantly and, forcing himself to breathe the noxious air, he was soon at the bottom of the ladder. He lowered a foot carefully to the tunnel floor. The liquid came halfway up his shins. It was flowing faster than he expected, but a bigger shock was its temperature. The sewage was warm. A pungent steam rose from the surface, swirling in clouds around the lantern, which was burning with an unusually bright flame. Montmorency remembered from the chemistry lectures at the Scientific Society how different gases burned with different colors and intensity. He wished he had paid more attention to the detail. Could he be in danger here? Like the miners he'd heard about who'd been suffocated by the buildup of a poison gas or buried alive when a stray spark set off an explosion. He was diverted from that problem when a sudden movement on the ledge to his left caught his attention just in time for him to see a rat's fat tail flicking out of range of his light. He might be the only human in the sewer, but he wouldn't be short of company.

As he walked, he drew a chalk line along the wall, so that he would be able to find his way back. When he reached a junction between two tunnels, he put an arrow to show which one he had taken. His mind rushed ahead. He decided that as he discovered where each entry shaft came down, he would chalk a symbol to remind him where he was on future journeys. He thought some up: *CX* for Charing Cross was an easy one. *PDY* for Piccadilly, perhaps. He realized that in spite of the smell, the dark, and the possible danger, he was still committed to this adventure. That being here, underground, was already taking on a special thrill for him. It was rather like being inside one of Doctor Farcett's diagrams of the structure of the lungs, the kidneys, or of the route of blood around the body. The tubes intersected like arteries and veins, the tunnels growing wider and higher as they took in more of London's liquids. When they came together into the biggest of all they had an awesome grandeur, yet each tiny brick in the wall was just as important as the whole: like a cell in a living thing.

He had promised himself he wouldn't go too far that night. He would go up a likely looking ladder, steal what he could, and get home as fast as possible. By his own reckoning he must be somewhere to the north of Trafalgar Square. There might be a shop stocking tobacco, fine lace, shoes, or something he could sell to help pay next week's rent.

Climbing out carefully, quietly, looking around all the time as he raised the lid, he realized that he was farther west, toward Mayfair, in an area of richer pickings. There before him was a jeweler's, its windows cleared of the most valuable merchandise, but with a few small trinkets still on display. In no time, he had broken the glass, taken what he could, and swung back down the hole. With one hand on the top of the ladder, he used the other to stuff his booty into his pockets, thrilled that he would have to sew extra pouches onto the inside of his clothes if his hauls were going to be this big.

He couldn't resist hanging on there, listening as the theft was discovered and excited voices organized a search of the local lanes and streets to find the culprit. Triumphant, he made his slimy, solitary journey home.

Hauling himself out of "his" manhole back in Covent Garden, Scarper was struck by the clarity of the air. He realized how bad he must smell, and looked down to see his trousers soaked with greasy sludge. He decided to do something about it. He needed a change of clothes for the morning, something to tide him over until he could get some money in exchange for the stolen jewels. A tramp was asleep on the steps of the Theatre Royal in Drury Lane. He was dirty and drunk, but he was dry, and had a sack of belongings at his side. Moments later, there was no sack, and the tramp slept on, unaware that he had lost everything except the clothes on his body.

Montmorency might have hopes of becoming a gentleman, but Scarper really wasn't a very nice man.

13. THE FLUSHERS

Scarper was feeling smugly pleased with himself after the success of his first job, but there were plenty of scares in those early days, constantly reminding him of the need for caution and of how much he still had to learn. For all the perils of navigating his way through the underground sludge, the most dangerous moments, from the point of view of being caught, came as he entered and left his manhole. He had to take special care not to be observed. Aboveground, that sometimes meant waiting in the shadows far longer than he'd have liked, to make sure that the last bystander had left. Below, it meant overcoming his enthusiasm to get home with his loot, and listening hard, teaching himself to recognize the street noises that told him a carriage, a pedestrian or, worst of all, a policeman had entered the street.

Quite soon, he learned that his romantic view of the sewers as parts of a body was right in more ways than one. The body could malfunction like any other living thing. When a human body developed blockages, doctors were called in, not always successfully. When the sewers silted up, they sent in the "flushers." Fortunately for the people of London, although the flushers were less well paid and less well respected than the medics, they had a far better record of putting things right.

Scarper's first encounter with the flushers came as he made a rare daytime trip to try to clarify in his mind the precise underground links between Green Park, Buckingham Palace, Pimlico and Vauxhall, where he thought there might be a possible escape route direct to the Thames for use in emergencies. Not being preoccupied with planning a theft, he was off guard, and quite enjoying the trip, when he was startled by the echo of a manhole cover being dragged away and the boom of coarse male voices.

There was a sudden burst of light from a shaft just ahead of him, and a harsh metallic thudding rang out as someone came down the metal steps. Scarper thought at once of the police and flattened himself into a recess in the wall in case he was spotted. But as the men came down, one after the other, it was clear they weren't looking for him. They were laughing and joking, carrying spades and buckets, as if they were on a bizarre day trip to an underground seaside. One of them, giving his mate a helping hand down the ladder, broke into a popular song, which echoed through the stinking caverns like a solo in a cathedral:

"Take my hand and let me lead you

To the garden, dear.

Honeysuckle scents the evening,

Smell the roses near.

Lavender enchants the senses,

Fragrant lilies, too.

Darling mine, break down your fences,

Let me be with you."

"Give it a rest, Bill!" complained his friend, pulling his hand away as he squelched down into the slurry. "We get the joke. Let's just knock out that blockage and get back out as quick as we can, right?"

The light from their lanterns cast huge shadow images of the men onto the walls of the tunnel as they swayed in their waders towards an intersection not far from Scarper's hiding place. Bill was whistling his tune now, as they fished out floating debris from the water and passed it back down the line to be put into a bucket on a rope and hauled back to the surface. One of the men lifted up what looked like an ancient pair of women's stays. He wrapped the dripping corset around his overalls and started to wiggle and pout like a dancer.

"Yeah, my granny had one of those!" called the next in line. "You look just like her, come to think of it — only fatter!"

"Well, I can't help being fat, can I? Every time I kiss your wife she gives me a biscuit!"

There was a scuffle as the husband playfully defended his wife's honor and, with the men's motion, the river of filth lapped up the walls, sloshing against Scarper. He stayed as still as he could and, amidst the banter, the flushers didn't notice him as they went about their work. The corset was passed back towards the steps, and the team set to work, attacking a huge cake of stinking mud that was blocking the way to the adjoining tunnel. They shoveled the mess into their buckets and passed them from hand to hand to be pulled up to the street. Now and again they would stop and hold up some new treasure they had unearthed. From his hideaway, Scarper marveled at how some of it could ever have gotten down there. The keys and coins might have been dropped down drains, but what was the story behind the chair that formed the main cause of the blockage, or the cricket bat that set off another round of horseplay among the men? There were boots and shoes, and (Scarper thought) something that was either a judge's wig or a dead cat. There were bottles, jars, assorted rags, and what might once have been a set of false teeth. It was a while since Scarper had felt sick in the sewers, but there was something about this last find that seriously turned his stomach.

As the flushers worked, Scarper felt the water level around his legs drop and the speed of the flow increase. They had stripped out one of London's arteries and, once the circulation was reestablished, they were away up the ladder, slamming the manhole back shut with a deafening crash.

Scarper was aware now that he didn't have this underworld all to himself. He would have to be careful when he was down there during the day, but the encounter gave him a new idea for avoiding trouble at street level. If he was ever challenged as he emerged from underground, he would simply smile and say, "I bet you're glad you haven't got my job.'"

14. THE PAPER

Scarper had been lucky to find Vi and Mrs. Evans. Neither of them was interested in cleaning, particularly at the top of the house, and he was left undisturbed in his room. Both of them enjoyed a wild social life at night. He didn't like to let himself imagine what they might be up to, but their chaotic lifestyle meant his own eccentric comings and goings could, for the time being at least, pass unremarked. Some of the other tenants really did work at the market, and rose early to unload goods coming into London from all over the country. Most of them, like Scarper, slept for much of the day. Others kept more regular hours, but there was no pattern and so much unexplained activity that there was no room for suspicion. Scarper knew from prison that people living at close quarters learn to turn a blind eye and a deaf ear to one another's activities. Only by believing that their neighbors are doing the same can they stay sane.

As he amassed more and more loot from the sewer raids, Scarper was getting increasingly irritated at having to continue a life of "ordinary" crime. He still needed to steal boots (from the docks), food (from the market), and a certain amount of cash; he found it demeaning to be operating like a common criminal when he was in possession of valuable goods that might finance a higher form of life, if he could only find a way of selling them without drawing attention to himself.

It was early morning, and he had just returned from a successful trip to Hampstead, where, in a substantial modern villa (built, he thought, for someone with more money than taste) he had found a grotesque but valuable silver tea set, laid out on display as if it were waiting for him. Stuffed into the bags and flaps he had sewn inside his jacket and trousers it had weighed him down on the long journey back, but now it was nestled safely under the floorboards, alongside his other trophies, ready to be sold when Montmorency got into action.

Perhaps it was time he did.

Scarper was tired. Lying on the grubby mattress, which smelled so strongly of previous tenants, he realized that the damp patch on the wall by the filthy window had grown since his arrival. He had noticed then that it looked like a map of Europe, with its irregular central splotch dotted around with islands. Now the long straight face of Portugal had grown a nose, and the Hebrides had multiplied as if there had been a volcanic eruption. Greece and Italy seemed to be moving towards a merger. He put his finger in the middle of the darkened plaster, somewhere around the ever-shifting borders of Serbia, Bosnia, and Herzegovina. It crumbled in a shower of powder, just as the countries themselves were doing, a thousand miles away. He was ready to move on from these grim lodgings. But now he needed rest, and by the dim light he lay and idly scanned his (stolen) newspaper.

Less than a hundred yards away, at the Bow Street Police Station, the same edition lay on the table, surrounded by gloomy men in dark blue uniforms. The headline leaped out at each of them:

POLICE HUMILIATED!

MORE JEWEL ROBBERIES AND STILL NO SUSPECTS
NEW CRIMINAL MASTERMINDS AT WORK, SAY
POLICE

By our special correspondent.

Sergeant Newman, his round face purple with anger, read
the article to his miserable force, spitting out the words. The
police constables' shoulders sank and their heads dropped as
the story unfolded.

Around the corner, Scarper sat up in bed as he read, allowing himself a surge of pride, like an actor reading a good review.

The Metropolitan Police stand shamed and mystified today, after three months of daring raids that have
seen shops, homes, and public institutions invaded and
robbed by a gang of criminals of such ingenuity that
they emerge from nowhere and disappear without trace.

My God, thought Scarper, *has it only been three months? I feel
as if I've been doing this all my life!*

Surely it's not as long as that, thought Constable Roberts. *It's
just coincidence — a few jobs here and there....*

Police arriving at the scene of one crime only moments
after the alarm was raised failed to find even the merest
clue. The victim, Matthew Barnadore, Esq., a goldsmith
in Holborn, was outraged at the failure of the authorities
to catch the culprits.

"I pay my taxes," he said, "and I expect a better service than this. The police could do nothing to help me.

Shopkeepers throughout the capital have been hit by this gang, and no property has been recovered."

Scarper shook his head as he recalled the raid. *I was lucky that time, got straight back down the hole. Heard the police before I was down the ladder. A couple more seconds and they'd have got me....*

Constable Roberts was indignant. "We got there as fast as we could. What more do they want?" he said.

Inspector Spier of Scotland Yard ...

Scarper was flattered that Scotland Yard was on the case.

"Scotland Yard!" Roberts hissed with contempt. "What do they know about anything? Call themselves detectives. They ought to work the beat like the rest of us."

Sergeant Newman ignored him and continued reading.

... could only respond with the assertion that London may be in the grip of some new criminal masterminds.

Scarper glowed. Constable Roberts stared at his boots.

"These people work as a team and coordinate their attacks in diverse areas to stretch our manpower to the limit. However, through diligent work our men are building up information on their operations ..."

Now Scarper was getting anxious. A constable stifled a giggle.

"... and we are confident that before too long we will have them under lock and key. The public must have patience. It will be rewarded." However ...

Sergeant Newman cleared his throat and slowed his pace.

> ... a police source has suggested to this correspondent ...

Here Constable Harris, one of Newman's most recent recruits, colored slightly and nervously brushed nonexistent crumbs from his uniform.

> ... that in truth the police are being made to look ridiculous, and have no idea who is behind these raids....

Scarper smiled. Sergeant Newman angrily scanned the faces of his team.

> It is possible that a gang from outside London or even overseas may be at work. "All we can do is watch the local dealers and wait for some of the stolen goods to turn up within the criminal fraternity," he said.

"I seem to remember those were my words at yesterday's beat meeting," hissed Sergeant Newman, throwing the paper down. "I WILL NOT HAVE MY MEN TALKING TO THE NEWSPAPERS!"

Constable Harris looked away and regretted accepting a beer from an inquisitive stranger in the pub the day before.

"Now, get back to your duties," barked Sergeant Newman, "and keep your wits about you!"

The policemen filed out onto the street, far from inspired. Scarper, energized by the report and relieved that he had not given in to the temptation to sell some of his silver at the local market, decided to go out for some breakfast before his nap. With the paper under his arm he strode happily along, doffing his cap to a line of miserable policemen coming from the other way.

15. Moving On

Scarper had a problem, and it was one he had foreseen long ago in his prison cell. His loot was so valuable that it could only be disposed of by the sort of person he was aiming to become. It was time for one last "common" burglary.

As Scarper made his way to Robert Farcett's house that Wednesday, he knew he was taking a chance. Would this still be the maid's day off? Would Doctor Farcett be out at one of his meetings, or would he spot his old patient, a man he could recognize from every scar on his body?

The front of the house was quiet. Around the back, the garden gate was, as before, unlocked. There were the French windows, shut, but not secured. Seconds later, he was in the doctor's study. It was a scene of industry on the verge of chaos. There were documents and journals everywhere, in piles that suggested a deliberate order, but each stack was on the point of tipping over into a messy heap on the floor. Scrunched-up balls of discarded paper circled the wastebasket. One or two had actually gone inside it. Diagrams and charts had been pinned to the front of the overfilled bookcases. Scarper was rather touched to see the heavily annotated image of his own injured body hanging among them, under the heading PRISONER 493.

The picture was beautifully drawn in fine lines of dark black ink. He was shown from the front and then, alongside, from the back. There were no features on his face, and a tiny loincloth had been drawn over his private parts. Every scar was marked: the long, jagged one down his back, the crumpled puncture mark beneath his shoulder, the sweeping cut under his ribs, and the long incision down his thigh. Every little scratch and scrape was there, alongside the deliberate wounds inflicted by the doctor in his efforts first to keep the body alive, and then to explore its capacity for recovery and repair.

A framed family photograph on the desk showed the doctor surrounded by young girls on the steps of a large country house. The distinguished-looking man in the wheelchair was, presumably, Farcett's father. (He had the same thin eyebrows and dimpled chin.) There was no sign of a mother. Too much childbirth perhaps? Could that be what had sent young Robert into medicine? Or had he sought a profession because the older boy (who was taller and fatter, with long side-whiskers, a pompous expression, and his hand on the old man's shoulder) was due to inherit the family wealth?

Scarper left the windows open, in case he had to get away in a hurry, and went upstairs. He needed clothes — a full set that would see him through his entrance into polite society. After opening a few wrong doors (one revealing a splendid flush lavatory with a pattern of blue flowers on the inside) he found the dressing room. Clearly the doctor had someone to organize his personal life, even if he couldn't control his own study, because the clothes were beautifully stacked, shirts with shirts, socks with socks, ties with ties. He found a large bag in a cupboard in the hall and carefully packed himself one of everything, right down to the underwear and the shoes.

When he had finished, the room looked untouched. He knew from the mess downstairs that the doctor himself was hardly likely to notice if anything was missing. He just hoped for the maid's sake that she wasn't too meticulous about counting the laundry; or that if she was, she had the sense not to mention any discrepancy to her master. While a tramp might be fairly resigned about losing his only clothes, an aristocrat would be furious if his second-best pants were missing.

On the way out, he took a chance and stopped in the study. He sat down at the desk, found a sheet of heavy notepaper and used the doctor's most stylish pen to write a brief note, straining to use the very best handwriting and spelling he could muster. It was to be the passport to his new life, but would also cover him if he were stopped while carrying Doctor Farcett's bag through the London streets.

The letter directed the manager of one of London's top hotels to provide a private room with a bath and a view of the park, for long-term occupation. The bearer of the message and the luggage — Scarper — was to wait there for the arrival of his master, who signed himself with a flourish:

16. THE MARIMION
HOTEL

The Marimion Hotel had been built as a grand private residence only a few years before by one of London's favorite party goers, a self-made shipping millionaire who had wanted to celebrate his success in a style everyone could see. Passersby had watched the delivery of fine marble and stone from all over the world, as the house — designed to mimic the most ostentatious aspects of almost every period of architecture — rose in its proud plot opposite Hyde Park. Magazines had carried long, illustrated articles about the interior decoration and soft furnishings just as the newspapers started to report concerns about the owner's business dealings and honesty. There was even some doubt about his real identity. The family never moved in, and the house was sold and turned into a hotel as its creator left the country to escape the scandal. It was the perfect place for Montmorency to begin his new life.

The manager, Mr. Longman, was just that: rather too tall, it seemed, for his own muscles to support, so that when he was tired or relaxed he appeared to fold down at all his main joints. His shoulders drooped forward, his hips back, and his loose wrists swung somewhere around his knees. He could stand straight, and when he did he made a smart and efficient host to his illustrious guests, but as he passed from the gentility of the lobby though the swing doors to the kitchens and storerooms, his appearance and behavior were transformed. He was a moody and untrusting boss, repeatedly accusing his staff of stealing food or skimping on the cleaning. New hotels were being built all over London, and cooks, maids, and porters didn't stay in their jobs at the Marimion any longer than they could help.

Some of them left because of Longman's daughter, Cissie, who was always hovering in the hotel, even though she had no particular role there. The more unkind chambermaids claimed that she was just hanging around waiting for a proposal from a rich American, and it was true that, glimpsing her from behind with her hat on, one or two guests had given her a second look. She had a fine body: tall, slender, and with none of her father's tendency to collapse, but when she turned around there was no escaping the snarling droop of her lip, the hairy lump on one side of her nose, and the unfortunate hair, which a kind friend had once described as "appealing," and which, as a consequence, had never been restyled to keep pace with her age. It sprayed out in crisp bunches on either side of her ample face: unnaturally yellow and held in place by tightly tied, garish ribbons, whose tips often dragged across her plate as she ate, depositing dribbles of soup, stew, or custard on her shoulders afterward. There was a joke among the waiters that guests need not be shown the menu. They could just take a look at Cissie's dress.

Although the Marimion had got off to an excellent start after all the publicity (good and bad) that had attended its opening, it wasn't the sort of place customers visited a second time. So with bookings down, Mr. Longman was pleased to read Montmorency's note and especially its reference to a long stay. He wasn't greatly taken with the manservant, Scarper, who struck him as rather grubby, but he let him into one of the larger rooms on the "park" frontage of the building, with instructions to use the back stairs in future.

Safely installed, Scarper set about preparing for the arrival of his boss. He locked the door, ran a bath, and laid out Doctor Farcett's clothes on the high four-poster bed. He crossed the room to stash the bag in a dark mahogany wardrobe. Each of the heavy doors of this giant closet had a full-length mirror on the inside, and as Scarper opened them, he caught sight of himself in his tattered clothes, his skin ingrained with prison and sewer dirt and his hair lank and greasy. If all went well, this was as bad as he would ever look. From now on, he was on the way up. The bath was hot. There was scented soap, pomades, and cologne, even a special shaving brush and razor. Scarper scrubbed, rubbed, scraped, and pummeled himself clean. Then he emptied the water from the tub and ran himself another bath, just to be sure the dirt was gone. Wrapped in towels warmed on the fat bathroom radiator, he wiped the steam from the mirror and shaved away any trace of stubble. He climbed into Robert Farcett's clothes. There were far more layers than he had ever worn, each with its attendant buttons, braces, clips, and ties. He struggled with the cufflinks for ages (finally understanding what servants were for) and then, straightening the jacket and tying the shiny shoes, he crossed to the mirrors again.

There he was. The new Montmorency.

On his way to the Marimion, he had stopped off at Scarper's room to collect some of his stolen riches. He decided to revisit the first jeweler's he had robbed to see if they would buy some things he'd picked up in another raid. It would be his first chance to try out the accent, words, and mannerisms he'd cultivated for the part. Most were lifted from Robert Farcett, of course, but other Scientific Society members had given him ideas for speech patterns, gestures, and little habits that would mark him out as a member of the educated upper classes. This was his first test. He hid Scarper's clothes, locked the door, and walked to the grand staircase with one hand in a pocket, just to show he wasn't trying to impress. He descended slowly, his free hand sliding down the polished marble banister, guiding him along a graceful curve into the lobby. He took great care not to meet the two pairs of eyes that were trained on him from below. As he reached the ground, Mr. Longman backed away from him, bowing and rubbing his hands together apologetically.

"Mr. Montmorency, I am so sorry I was not here to greet you personally when you arrived. I cannot think what happened. I beg your pardon. I will have champagne sent up to your room."

"No matter, no matter," Montmorency replied in Doctor Farcett's voice. "You will find I make few demands. My man understands my needs and will see to them for me. I trust I will enjoy privacy in my room. I am going out now."

As he left, surprised to find the thick carpet reminding him of the grass outside the prison on the day of his release, he turned to deliver his first ever command to a servant, "Just leave the champagne outside the door at about eight o'clock, will you?"

Cissie Longman's mustache was positively twitching at the possibilities she saw for herself and this handsome new arrival at the Marimion.

17. THE RESIDENT GUEST

Walking to Mayfair, Montmorency concentrated on his every movement. As Scarper, he kept his shoulders up and his head down and forward, not broadcasting his presence or inviting an approach, but able through an upward flick of the eyeballs to observe everyone around him. Robert Farcett always kept his head up and his shoulders firmly down above a straight back. His chest and chin were held outward, and he walked in a way that expressed his entitlement to be where he was, and to go where he was going, the feet planted firmly one in front of the other at a steady, unhurried pace. Scarper had a roll to his walk, bobbing from side to side, and looking as if he had his hands in his pockets even when he didn't. That was his natural way of moving, but in Farcett's clothes Montmorency found imitation of the doctor easier than it had been when he'd tried to mimic him before. Balancing the top hat proved a little difficult at first, and though he knew he should touch it with his hand when he passed a lady, he feared that he might send it rolling into the road.

As he walked along, he cast his eyes to the side to see if he could catch a glimpse of his reflection in windows he passed. He checked the full effect approaching the jeweler's and cleared his throat, ready to say the words he had been practicing in

Scarper's little room for the past three months — "I wonder if you might take a look at these for me?" He felt into his pocket, ready to pull out a pearl necklace and matching set of earrings stolen from the other side of town.

His hand was shaking as he opened the shop door, but he stared steadily towards the shopkeeper, not quite engaging his eyes. Demanding attention in the way that prison guards and scientists had demanded attention of him, but cutting off any inquiry beyond those necessary for the deal to take place.

"I wonder if you might take a look at these for me?"

Would the disguise work? Had he made some elementary mistake in his dress or manner that would send the jeweler running for the police? It seemed an endless wait for a response but, in fact, it was only long enough for the tradesman to draw breath and clasp his hands in the gesture of subservience Montmorency had seen directed towards him only once before — from Longman at the Marimion that very day.

"Certainly, sir. If I may ..."

The jeweler took the necklace and examined it with his spyglass, commenting on the quality of the pearls and the delicacy of the clasp.

"Delightful. Quite delightful."

"They have been in the family for some time."

"Certainly sir, I quite understand. I am sure we can come to some arrangement. I was thinking of a figure in the region of fifty guineas."

Montmorency was enjoying himself now and put on an air of disappointment.

"As I say, I am reluctant to see them go."

"I might be able to stretch to sixty...."

Montmorency pursed his lips, and the jeweler looked down his magnifying glass again.

"The workmanship is excellent. Seventy guineas, sir."

"That seems agreeable." Montmorency was proud of the way he slightly slurred that last word, turning the *r* into a *w*.

"Yes, sir. Seventy guineas. I think we are agreed."

And so the deal was done. The jeweler was delighted with the transaction and charmed by his new customer who, he secretly imagined, must need the cash to pay off glamorous gambling debts. Montmorency was pleased, too. Once the jeweler had visited his safe and handed over the money, he bought some cuff links that looked easier to fasten than Doctor Farcett's and, remembering not to sound too grateful as he took his leave, returned to the hotel. There, he settled the bill for his first week at the Marimion in advance, stifling any suspicions Longman may have had. The next priority was an extra set of clothes for Scarper: nothing flashy, just plain, clean working clothes of the sort such a servant might wear. Scarper went out to buy them himself while Montmorency "rested" at the Marimion.

Over the next few months a comfortable pattern was established. Most nights, Scarper quietly slid away from the hotel and made for the little room in Covent Garden. There he would change into his sewer clothes and set off for work. By now he had acquired a fine array of tools. His favorite was a lamp he could strap to his forehead leaving both hands free, but he blessed the day he had stolen, on a whim, a set of S-shaped hooks from a butcher's shop. These were now attached to the ladder in the manhole shaft and, from them, hung spare lamps and a pair of thigh-high waterproof boots, taken from a sleepy boatman. To Scarper's eye they wouldn't have looked out of place on a member of the royal family fishing for salmon in the River Spey. When Scarper returned from a raid, he changed back into his street clothes and made off for the Marimion, slipping up the back stairs with a quick nod to any of the hotel staff he ran into, and a raised eyebrow implying, "Must get back. The master's waiting upstairs and I'm late!" Within minutes, the bath taps were running and, in a cloud of scented steam, Scarper was transformed once more into Montmorency.

Montmorency had new garments, too. On that first night in the hotel he had looked in wonder at the inside of the wardrobe with its lines of hanging rails and hooks, its special sliding trays for shirts, shallow drawers for socks and underwear, deeper ones for he knew not what, and little compartments for collar studs. He had wondered how it was possible for anyone to fill so much space. He'd even felt a surge of envious contempt for those who could. Now it was brimming with things of his own, all bought legitimately from some of London's foremost outfitters.

Montmorency had discovered a streak of vanity in himself. He enjoyed looking grand, even though, still cautious, he left the hotel only to shift Scarper's stolen goods and to buy essentials for them both. The rest of the time he paraded in front of the mirror, practicing phrases and actions he'd observed in other guests. He read books, including one on etiquette (which he had wrapped in brown paper for disguise). He kept up with the newspapers, and manicured his nails. Sometimes, after a hard night's work as Scarper, he lay in bed all day in his silk pajamas, refusing to answer the door.

18. $\mathscr{C}$ISSIE

There were complications. Most notably Cissie, whose fantasies had been fed by Montmorency's secrecy and silence, which she interpreted as smoldering charm. She seemed to be everywhere. Leaning provocatively on the marble banisters as he went downstairs; lolling longingly on a chaise longue in the lobby when he passed; showing just a little too much ankle when he was near, and twiddling her frizzy hair between her stubby fingers. Montmorency had a break from her attentions when a famous actor came to stay. But his play folded after a week, and she turned to Montmorency again with even more intensity, as if to make up for her treachery. He overheard her father berating her for having ideas above her station. After that she was keener still. She accosted him in the corridor, her piggy eyes cast down, her large foot playfully pawing at the carpet as she talked in a squeaky lisp.

"Mithter Montmorenthy, have you seen my likkle kittin?"

Montmorency wondered for a moment what language she was speaking.

"My likkle kittin. She'th lotht. Thilly Thithie'th lotht her likkle kittin!"

"Oh, dear. I'm so sorry. I'll keep my eye open for her."

"She'th stwypee with a likkle likkle sthtar of white bwetween her eerth."

"Then she shouldn't be too difficult to find. I must go."

"But where do you think sthe might be? You're tho thophithti-cated, you mutht be able to think of thum̦where."

"Have you checked the washing?"

"Oh *no*!" She raised her wrist to her forehead in a theatrical gesture of despair. "Are you thaying that she'th been stwrangled by a theet?"

"No. I'm suggesting that you look in the washing basket. Cats like climbing inside things, you know." He made a move towards the stairs, trying not to seem too impolite. "Good day!"

But Cissie danced into his path. "Oh, Mithter Montmorenthy, you know tho much about animalth! Will you help me look for my likkle kittin?"

"Not now, I'm afraid I have business to see to." He tried to step around her, but she carried on wheedling, refusing to move.

"Of course you mutht get to your busineth, if itth more pwr-ething than Thithie'th likkle kittin stwrangled in the wathing. Are you thure you can't thpare a likkle minute to therch for my likkle kittin with me?"

"Well, perhaps just a minute, but surely one of the staff, or your father could …" He looked around in the hope of spotting a chambermaid or a porter who could take over.

"Do you know what my thuthpithion is?"

Montmorency was suddenly on the alert, once he'd worked out that she'd used the word "suspicion." Now he was anxious to ensure that nobody was near enough to hear in case she had sensed something odd about him and was about to say something incriminating. But he needn't have worried. At least not about his secret being discovered.

"My thuthpithion ith that sthe hath thneaked into your room! Thall we stherch it together?"

"I don't think so," gasped Montmorency, as her face loomed closer to his, and she made a grab for his hand.

He was saved when her lurch towards him revealed the likkle kittin, who was left behind on the carpet where Cissie had hidden her under her petticoats. (Contrary to Cissie's opinion, Montmorency didn't have much of an affinity with animals. Even so, he could have sworn that the little kitten flashed him a look of sympathetic exasperation and disgust.)

"There she is!" he said, gently maneuvering Cissie away from him.

"Oh, Mithter Montmorenthy! You have found Thithie'th likkle kittin! I knew I could twutht you to wrethcue her from dithathter! You are tho marvelloth. I could kith you!"

Montmorency flinched.

"But I weally muthent, mutht I?" she added, her hands clasped behind her, and her foot drawing out circles on the floor. "It would be motht untheemly! I thuppothe I can let you kith *me* though, if you weally mutht!"

She tilted her face towards him and closed her eyes. He picked up the kitten, placed it on her shoulder, turned, and strode away. He didn't look back, but in the ornate mirror at the end of the hall he caught a glimpse of the animal licking enthusiastically at the gravy on her neck.

Montmorency's instinct was to ignore Cissie, but he knew the problem had to be dealt with. Cissie could get hold of the master key, and he suspected that she was entering his room when he was out. He hoped it was just for romantic schoolgirlish purposes: to steal a hair from his brush, or sniff his sheets, but he couldn't risk her finding any evidence that could later be used against him. He became obsessively tidy, so that any disturbance of his things would be obvious, and was always careful and cool in her presence, determined not to give her hope. That only made her more ardent. One day she asked his advice, approaching him with such gravity that he thought there must have been a death in the family. Should she wear the pink ribbons or the orange ones? (Actually, she said "fuchsia" and "tangerine.") When he replied, "Both," with a contempt she failed to notice, she did wear them both for a week, tied so tightly that her pigtails stood out almost at right angles, like hairy ice-cream cones.

Montmorency, for all his criminal blood, was not a violent man. He wanted to strangle her.

Instead he planned a diversion. Perhaps if she experienced unwanted attentions herself, she would stop lavishing them on him. He decided that Scarper would make a play for her. He was on his way out one night when he saw Cissie slumped against the wall outside the kitchen, greedily finishing off some pudding left uneaten by one of the guests. She was totally engrossed, the bowl only an inch or so from her mouth, and the spoon shoveling away with a brisk, rhythmical scrape. Scarper didn't bother with winning glances, flattery, or flirtation. He crept up to Cissie just before she started licking the last remains, and placed his hands to either side of her on the wall. It was the backstairs version of her ambush of Montmorency in the corridor, only there she had pinned him down with his own politeness.

"Fancy a walk?"

She clasped the dirty bowl to her bosom as if it was her pudding he was after, adding to the pattern of food stains on her dress.

"Shut up and let me go, you horrible man," she growled in a voice completely unrelated to the baby-speak she used for Montmorency.

"Come on, I know you want it."

"Do you think I'd have anything to do with the likes of you, you brute?"

She pushed against him trying to break free, and raised her face to his, the fumes from her rotting teeth cutting through the sickly sweetness of the creamy confection.

Scarper felt a shudder of danger. Would she see the resemblance between himself and his master? He took her by the chin, and yanked her head to one side, giving his own cheek a brush from the wiry frizz, but letting him whisper into her grimy ear.

"If I catch you in my master's room, you know what you'll get."

He wasn't quite sure what he meant, but it was clear that she thought she did, and he knew that she wouldn't be visiting again. He pushed her away roughly and left by the back door. The stare of contempt burning into his back was as strong as any of the looks of love that afflicted Montmorency.

19. MR. LYONS

Cissie apart, life at the Marimion was calm, possibly a little too calm for Montmorency. He had already started traveling more. London had only so many jewelers prepared to buy high-value goods for cash, and Montmorency was anxious not to become too well known by them. Scarper was getting better at his job. The loot was richer, but also more recognizable, particularly if a raid had made the papers. So once or twice a week, Montmorency would take a train (first class, of course), far enough out of London to dilute suspicion. He went to Bath (plenty of shops, and even the thrill of an auction house), Guildford, Cheltenham, Dorchester, and Oxford. Seeing people going about their daily enterprises gave him a taste for more action.

He started mingling with the upper-class men he had been imitating, pretending to himself at first that it was all in the cause of research. He hung around cab ranks, eavesdropping on their conversations hearing their voices shift with the wave of an elegant cane from languid musings on society gossip to clipped orders to the drivers to make for glamorous locations all over London. He wanted to know what happened when they got out of the cabs and strode into the parties and theaters that played such an important part in their lives. He decided to go to the opera.

The huge bulk of the opera house rose above the Strand on a small hill. Its grim rear end sat down on the cobbles and barrows of the flower market. The pillars on its grand frontage smirked like teeth towards the narrow lanes and courtyards where Scarper lived. Mrs. Evans's tenants included Charlie, an aging tenor who occasionally got a part in the chorus, and Albert, a burly romantic who sometimes helped out backstage. Their irregular hours helped cover up Scarper's unusual comings and goings, and he often heard them discussing a performance, or whistling some of the tunes as they returned in the early hours. Mrs. Evans and Vi had links with the opera, too. They would dress up in the evenings, as the humble poverty of the area gave way to the arrival of carriages, cabs, and the raucous braying of the rich. They watched the audience arrive and leave. Sometimes they would bring men back with them. Sometimes they would be gone all night. Scarper didn't ask questions. He didn't want them asking questions of him. But he fancied having a look at what went on when glitter briefly overlaid the filth.

He consulted his book of etiquette to see what he should wear. Although he had a fine selection of day clothes, he had not yet needed evening wear, and set off for one of his favorite locations: a tailor's shop near Regent Street. He had been nervous on his first visit, afraid that he was risking discovery. Would he let something slip that might send the shopkeeper to the police? Would he have to explain the scars that he couldn't hope to conceal? Then he came to understand that the relationship between a tailor and his client had all the intimacy of the confessional, and he began to look forward to his encounters with Mr. Lyons, a craftsman of distinction, but nevertheless a tradesman who knew his place.

He opened the door, setting off a little brass bell that brought the tailor scurrying from his workshop.

"Mr. Montmorency. Always a delight to see you, sir. Come in, come in. I'll get your box."

Mr. Lyons pulled back a thick woven curtain and motioned Montmorency to an armchair, while he reached up to a shelf piled high with cardboard boxes. Each was labeled with a code word that referred to a particular customer without giving the information away to anyone else. Montmorency's tag was MCYMRN, which he had deciphered as most probably standing for "Montmorency, Marimion": The customer and the delivery address summed up in six short letters, and curiously reminiscent of that chalk code Scarper had used in his early days in the sewers, long since rubbed away.

"Quite a little treasure trove we've got here now," said Lyons, taking off the lid to reveal a selection of buttons and samples of fabrics and trimmings, which told the story of Montmorency's growing wardrobe, and meant his clothes could be replaced, mended, or matched with the minimum of fuss. At the bottom were sheets of paper listing Montmorency's measurements in tiny writing, with an occasional crossing out and correction showing how the good life was beginning to fill him out.

"What's it to be today, sir?"

"Evening wear. I'm going to the opera."

"Anything in particular, sir?"

"Everything." Montmorency was suddenly worried. Would it seem strange that he hadn't any evening clothes already? He noticed the tailor's notes, patted his stomach and added, "I seem to be spreading a bit, you know."

"I thought I might be needing my tape measure when you walked in, sir, to tell the truth. The Marimion's kitchen must be very good."

"Well, I'm in your hands," said Montmorency. Then he rose, removed his jacket and spread his arms as he had so often for Doctor Farcett. But where Doctor Farcett had been tongue-tied on these occasions, the tailor seemed to find the lack of eye contact and the distraction of his task a spur to speech.

"Some of my gentlemen have been going for a slighter, longer trouser this season, sir. They like the hem to break right at the front of the shoe, just before the toes ... and I have some rather delightful red silk for the lining of the cape."

"I'll trust your judgment."

Mr. Lyons liked Montmorency. Some of his customers came in with fixed ideas of what they wanted, and then quibbled when the finished garment didn't suit them. He liked the way Montmorency — while clearly appreciating quality work and materials — left the big decisions to him. Most of all he liked the way Montmorency paid in cash, on the spot. There were plenty of others he could mention (but wouldn't, of course) who owed him considerable sums.

"Terrible business at old Lady Bevington's last night, sir." Mr. Lyons's little bald head, dotted with a spray of freckles, bounced about around Montmorency's knees.

"Oh? I hadn't heard."

"Robbery. They think it's that gang again."

Montmorency was confused. Scarper had had a night off for once, exhausted after a tricky job at a museum.

"The thing is, she was there — on her own, except for her maid who was asleep in the attic. She was leaving for Paris today. Now they say she's too weak to go. Scared witless she was. They caught one of them, though. No ordinary burglar. Some sort of crazed madman. Her son came home unexpectedly and found him sitting in the drawing room staring at her. They say her face was frozen with fear."

"Appalling," said Montmorency. He was actually a little sorry for Lady Bevington, but also contemptuous of the burglar who had let himself be caught doing what should have been a pretty straightforward break-in, and slightly annoyed that someone else was operating in his territory.

"Still," Lyons continued, "if they've got the ringleader of that gang that's been causing all the trouble, perhaps we can all sleep easier in our beds, sir."

"Indeed, we can," said Montmorency, inwardly relieved that the police thought they had cracked their case.

"What's the opera, sir?" Lyons caught Montmorency off guard with the question.

"Well... I hadn't actually decided."

"Oh, *Traviata,* sir! All my gentlemen say you must see *La Traviata.* Wonderful tunes, apparently. It's all about a courtesan with consumption. Falls in love and dies."

The tailor was behind him now, gently pressing the tape measure against his shoulders and down the center of his back. Every now and then, Montmorency caught a glimpse of a freckled finger dancing around his collar. Lyons kept up the chatter, interspersing the gossip with little reminders to himself of the shape of the proposed suit.

"Tell you what... (twenty-four and a half) ... I'll send my boy, Ned ... (seventeen, tuck and dart) ... around to find out when it's on. Now, let's see, I can have this suit ready for ... (standard hem, back split and pleat) ... a week from Monday. How about I send him around for a ... (sixteen and a half) ... ticket for the first performance after that, and we can put it on your bill?"

"And a little bit for your trouble."

"Oh, it's no trouble, sir. Not for you. But that's very kind, sir, very kind."

Montmorency suddenly found himself overwhelmed by the urge to confide in Lyons. This was the only human being who ever deliberately touched him now, and for years before only the doctor and the members of the Scientific Society had come so close. Their rough, impersonal mauling was quite unlike the deft care of the tailor, who was the only person with whom he had anything approaching a normal conversation these days.

"Can I tell you something, Lyons?"

"Of course, sir … (three, overlap and lining)."

"I've never been to the opera before."

Lyons — who was around the front again now, measuring Montmorency's outside leg — looked up with a hint of a wink.

"I thought so, sir. I had a feeling you were from out of town. Don't worry. We'll see you're all right."

Montmorency was touched by his tailor's concern, but alerted to a danger, too. He hadn't completely mastered London manners yet, and if this tradesman, who was on his side, could spot the signs, how much more might a policeman see? How easily might an ill-considered gesture or a clumsy expression raise a small doubt that might grow into suspicion?

"Now, you'll be needing a new hat, sir. They have a special kind for the opera. You can squash them down to put them under your seat." Montmorency detected a new, more patronizing tone in Lyons's voice. "Otherwise the person behind wouldn't be able to see, you see, sir. May I recommend Mr. Rigby next door? Does a very fine line in opera hats. A very fine line indeed. I'm all finished with the measuring, sir. A fitting on Thursday?"

"Excellent. I'll come in after lunch."

Until now, Montmorency had relied upon the hat he had taken from Doctor Farcett's house on that Wednesday afternoon six months before. After his early awkwardness balancing it on his head, he now felt uncomfortable without it. It looked good, and it was useful, too, as he found minutes later when he turned it upside down and dropped his gloves into it on the counter of the hatter's shop.

20. AT THE HATTER'S

Mr. Rigby, the hatter, stood at the door of his shop, drumming his fingers on the glass and looking out at the street. He noticed Montmorency leaving the tailor's, judged him to be well off, and in need of a new hat, and when he saw him making towards his own shop he was glad that his friend and neighbor, Lyons, had sent him a new customer. Rigby was very thin, very smart, and very obsequious. He had a habit of fidgeting with his long nimble fingers, rapping on the counter or waving his arms and flicking at the air, as if he were playing some invisible keyboard and conducting an orchestra as he spoke. *Freakshow would have loved this,* thought Montmorency, and for a moment he was transported back to his prison cell, where his old companion had taught him to notice such idiosyncrasies.

"Ah, sir," Rigby said with the hint of a bow. "What can I do for you, sir? I don't believe I've had the honor of serving you before."

"I need an opera hat." Montmorency was excited by the prospect of finding out exactly how the collapsible hats worked. But he didn't want to demonstrate his ignorance, and left it up to the shopkeeper to do the talking.

"I'll show you our latest model." Rigby wheeled a dark wooden set of steps to a shelf where boxes no more than three inches high were stacked one on top of the other. He climbed up, then turned to get an aerial view of Montmorency's head and judged the size with an experienced eye. "Yes, seven and a half, I believe."

Rigby carried the box down, holding it with just the tips of his fingers. Placing it gently on the counter, he slid back his cuffs like a magician about to do a trick and lifted the lid. Inside lay a thick black pancake of silk. Using the edges of his two thumbs Rigby lifted it, and with a sharp gesture reached under the brim with his middle fingers.

Thwhopp went the hat, and the crown popped up to form a shiny topper.

Montmorency felt a pang of childish joy, and the hatter looked at him with a face full of triumph. "Wonderful springs!" he cried, aglow with pride in the toy. He went on to show Montmorency how the mechanism worked, and how, despite the springs, the hat, when open, was as elegant as any other. He stroked the silk plush material as lovingly as if it had been a favorite cat. He brought down other hats to show how, when sprung open, this opera hat was almost indistinguishable from its everyday cousin. By the time he had finished, Montmorency had ordered himself not only the opera hat itself, but three others for daily wear: two black, and one gray. They were to be delivered to the Marimion that very afternoon, and he couldn't wait to get back to try them on. He was as happy as he had been since his first night down the sewers.

As he turned to go, the hatter called after him. "Sir. Forgive me, sir, but you seem to have forgotten your own hat, sir."

Montmorency looked around to see Rigby's face suddenly crumpling in bewilderment. He was examining the hat carefully, pulling back the leather band inside the brim.

"Why, this is one of ours! An old model. We gave up doing these four or five years ago when we got a new supplier for the silk."

Montmorency sensed danger. He was right.

"Good Heavens! It's one of Doctor Farcett's. He's been a customer here ever since his father brought him in for his first hat."

Montmorency could hear the blood pounding in his ears. In less than a second a dozen possibilities passed through his mind. Farcett might walk in at any moment just by chance and recognize him. Rigby might sense that the hat was stolen and report him to the police. He himself might blurt out something that blew his cover. Instead he found himself saying, "How extraordinary. How can you tell?"

Rigby beckoned him closer and showed him a tiny mark underneath the band. "That's my sign for him. We have symbols for the customers, for the makers, and if we ever get anything in for repair, we make a note of that, too. I'll be making up a sign for you, too, sir, after you've gone. I'll do something with the *M* and the *Y* of your name probably. You'll know where to look when the hats are delivered. Most of our customers probably don't realize there's anything there at all. So will you be seeing Doctor Farcett, sir, or do you want me to hold on to this in case he pops in?"

Montmorency tried to sound casual. "Oh, I'll give it back myself. After all, he's probably got mine! A mix-up somewhere, no doubt."

"Well, I'll mention it to him if I see him, sir," said Rigby affably.

All Montmorency could manage was a strangled smile. *I bet you will,* he thought to himself, as he left quickly.

So, after the brief comfort of hearing from the tailor that the police might be slackening off, he now had the prospect of Robert Farcett alerted to his movements. And it was his own fault. If he hadn't ordered those extra hats he would never have had to give his name. He could have just picked up the opera hat and walked away. Now someone was in possession of two pieces of his personal jigsaw. And there was nothing he could do about it.

He lay on his bed in the Marimion, flicking the opera hat open and closed, as miserable now as he had been happy before. He hated this feeling of gloom that sat in the center of his chest, making every breath an effort. The sudden reminder about the doctor had alerted him to every scar. Aches and twinges he hadn't felt for ages resonated through his body. With each movement of the hat he took stock of his situation, trying to console himself that things might not be as bad as they seemed.

Thwhopp. He was settled at the Marimion. Good.

Thwhopp. Scarper's rooms were secure. No one bothered him there. Good.

Thwhopp. The police seemed no nearer to catching him. Good.

Thwhopp. But bad, too, because the public and politicians were growing impatient for an end to the thefts.

Thwhopp. They had arrested Lady Bevington's burglar. Good.

Thwhopp. Gossip already pinned the other thefts on that man. Good.

Thwhopp. There was enough stuff under the floorboards at Scarper's to keep him going for some months. Good.

Thwhopp. If he lay low for a while the police would relax. Good.

Thwhopp. His victims might drop their guard. Good.

Thwhopp. It could be a sort of holiday. Good.

Thwhopp. And when he got back to work it would be easier than ever. Good.

Thwhopp. But the doctor might hear about his hat. Bad.

Thwhopp. The hatter knew Montmorency's name. Bad.

Thwhopp. He knew where he lived. Bad. Bad.

Thwhopp. Farcett might come and discover him. Bad. Bad. Bad.

Thwhopp. Expose him as a thief and a fraud. Bad. Bad. Bad. Bad.

Thwhopp. But ...

He lay still for a while, as the beginnings of an idea took hold. The tightness around his chest started to ease, and the vacuum of despair inside him began to fill with excitement. He could put things right. He just had to get the details straight. He had a plan.

Good.

Thwhopp.

21. In the Pub

He needed to eat and he needed to think, and he didn't fancy doing that in the restaurant at the Marimion with its attentive waiters and posing guests. So he changed into Scarper's clothes and slipped down the back stairs, Cissie diving from the hallway into the kitchen as he passed. He walked to Covent Garden, and back to the pub where he had eaten his first meal after leaving prison. The filthy barmaid was gone and, anyway, he would pay this time. He settled down with his pie, his pint, and the paper, which was trumpeting the news of Lady Bevington's burglary.

It was a more lurid account than the tailor's, with several quotes from her son about how he had returned unexpectedly to find his mother seated in an armchair, ashen with horror. He'd noticed a sack of jewels and silverware on the floor, and beside it, a one-legged man, snarling like an animal or the devil himself.

Scarper realized at once. It was Freakshow. He could imagine how the aging amateur crook, tempted perhaps as a result of their late-night chats about how to get rid of valuable loot, had gotten out of his depth and strayed into Lady Bevington's house on impulse. He pictured him struggling with the sack and his crutch, panicking when Lady Bevington appeared in person, and trying desperately to keep her quiet by making some of his famous faces. He must have been ready to abandon the sack and make an undignified getaway when the son had arrived and called the police.

The pub door opened and a group of policemen walked in. Scarper wasn't the only customer whose muscles instinctively tightened on seeing them, but it was clear in an instant that they were off duty, relaxed, and happy.

"I'll get this round, lads," said Sergeant Newman. "Roberts, Harris. What are you having?"

It was pints all around, and the landlady was impressed by what was obviously unusual generosity in the sergeant.

"Celebrating?" she asked.

"I'll say we are. Madam, you are looking at the team that's put a stop to all these burglaries. Harris here is the very man who arrested the perpetrator in the early hours of this very morning."

"I seen it in the paper. Can't have been very hard. They say he's only got one leg."

"That, madam, was the secret of his success."

"You see," said Roberts, taking up the story, "we were looking for a gang, or a master of crime. This guy's got the perfect cover. Not known for top-class jobs — been inside, but only for pickpocketing and suchlike."

"And we were looking for an athlete," said Newman. "Or a team of people who could slide in and out without being noticed. We wouldn't have given a cripple a second look. And it's no use looking for footprints when there's no foot."

Harris got back in. "Mind you, he can move fast. You should see him on that crutch of his, and how he can swing himself around and hop about even when you take it off him."

"And another thing," added Harris. "Came out of prison a year ago." He paused for effect. "Just when these burglaries started."

They all nodded as if Harris had had a stroke of genius.

"It's him, all right. All fits together." The sergeant lifted his glass. "Yes, I'm proud to say that the people of London can all sleep a little more sweetly in their beds. He's in the cells, and he'll be in court before you know it. And after what he's done to Lady B., he'll swing."

Scarper flinched at the idea of Freakshow hanging for his crimes. But he was comforted by the sight of Newman and his men, rejoicing in their imagined triumph and off his tail at least for a while. Yet in the back of his mind, an alarm bell was ringing. If harmless old Freakshow might die, what hope would there be for him if he should ever be caught? It was more important than ever to cover his tracks. He returned to the matter of the doctor and the hat.

As he walked away from the pub, he bumped into Mrs. Evans and Vi, decked out in their flamboyant but grubby dresses, their cheeks bright with rouge and their hair piled up in frizzy curls, ready for a night outside the opera house. They greeted him with girlish giggles, and he smiled back, secretly grateful to them for giving him an extra twist to his plan.

22. SORTED

Once he overcame his initial despair, he broke the problem down into its component parts. The hat itself was not the main difficulty. It was the hatter. It didn't really matter whether Farcett got back his hat or not, so long as the hatter said nothing. In the pub, Scarper had briefly toyed with the notion of putting a permanent end to the risk by killing Mr. Rigby, but back in the Marimion, Montmorency knew that such behavior was out of the question, and he despised Scarper for even entertaining the idea. He wanted a more clever solution, and one that was simple enough not to create new problems of its own.

The new hats that had been delivered from Rigby's sat in their boxes in a corner of Montmorency's room. He took one out and replaced it with Farcett's. Alongside he put a note, addressed to the doctor, saying simply:

Taken in error.

Apologies.

It was unsealed and unsigned. He didn't mind if the hatter read it. In fact, he rather hoped he would. He then wrote another note, to Rigby himself.

Dear Rigby,

I feel it would be appropriate for you to return this to its owner, after all. A matter of some delicacy is involved. I am sure I can count on your discretion.

M.

This was sealed. He wanted Rigby to be impressed by the confidentiality of the transaction.

A moment later, he called the porter, and sent him with the package and the note to the hat shop. Then he came to the part of the plan of which he was most proud and, somewhere deep in his conscience, most ashamed. He wrote another note to the hatter, this time in different handwriting, deliberately less careful of his spelling and style. The next morning he ran into Cissie on the stairs.

"Ah, Miss Longman," he said. "I wonder if you could do me a favor."

He beckoned her over to the corner and spoke in a conspiratorial tone.

"There is a matter of some urgency I need to deal with, and I need help from someone on whom I can rely absolutely."

Cissie was flattered and delighted at the implication that this was something Scarper could not be asked to do.

"I want you to deliver a letter. It contains a sum of money, and it is most important that it does not go astray. I will not need a reply. Your word that it has been safely delivered will be sufficient."

Cissie glowed at having his trust.

"To be honest with you, Miss Longman ... Cissie, I am slightly embarrassed about this ... about not having had enough money with me to pay yesterday. So don't make a big song and dance about handing it over. I'm sure you understand."

"Oh, yes," whispered Cissie, who was already planning to wear a veil over her hat. "I won't say a word."

He slipped the envelope into her hand. She looked at the address. It was sweet and typically noble of Mr. Montmorency to be so punctilious about paying his bills, and just like him to be shy about it. She went to her room for her coat and left with the air of a spy on a secret mission.

Cissie resisted the temptation to open the letter. It was a matter of honor not to, and she fought her natural inquisitiveness all the way to the shop. So she never knew that there was no money inside. She never knew that what the letter said was this:

I believe a gentleman may have returned to you a hat belonging to another gentleman. Their hats were accidentally exchanged in circumstances which, if known, could bring dishonor to them both, and to myself. I beg you, sir — for the sake of the two gentlemen, if not for myself — never to mention the matter to either of them or to anyone else. Great harm could be done by a careless word.

It was unsigned.

As Cissie sidled up to the shop, Rigby was at the window, tapping on the pane and surveying the street. He saw her coming, and judged from a distance the kind of woman she was. "No better than she looked" was the phrase that came to mind most readily. He expected her to turn towards the pub on the corner and was surprised when she made for his door. She passed the note over quickly and without a word. He read it as she walked away. It confirmed his assessment of her character and lifestyle. No better than she looked indeed. But the letter put both Montmorency and Farcett up in his estimation. Who would have thought that the doctor would have such a racy private life? Good for him. He deserved a bit of fun, and his secret would be safe with Rigby. The hat could wait at the back of the shop in case it were ever called for. Rigby expected it to stay there for a very long time.

As Montmorency made his way for his fitting at the tailor's on Thursday, he caught sight of Rigby at the window of his shop. The glass was dotted with fingerprints: a testament to the hatter's harmless little habit. Rigby raised an eyebrow and tapped his nose confidentially. Montmorency knew then that Cissie had played her part well, and everything would be all right.

Inside the tailor's, Mr. Lyons ran his freckled hands over the cutout pieces of Montmorency's opera suit. He seemed to get a physical pleasure out of handling fabric of such luxurious quality. Each section was chalked with the special symbols of the tailor's trade, ready to be sewn up after it had been pinned together. Montmorency stripped down to his underwear, and Lyons got down to work. As always he chatted — mumbling a bit as he held pins in his mouth — but keeping up a stream of gossip and opinion.

"Did you hear, sir? Lady Bevington passed away. They say it was the shock of that robber."

"Oh, dear," said Montmorency.

Lyons took this as a natural expression of sympathy for the old lady, but Montmorency was thinking of Freakshow, and how he would definitely face the gallows now.

"Of course," said Lyons, "an old lady like that would be easily scared. Not like you, sir. You'd have seen the varmint off, I'm sure. You being a military man and all."

"What's that?"

"You were in the army, weren't you, sir? I mean, I couldn't help noticing …" With an understanding smile, he pointed to the lumpy scar along the back of Montmorency's leg, and the purple blotch on his arm where his elbow had been smashed and repaired.

Montmorency thought the best policy was to go along with the idea, but he did his best to ward off further inquiries.

"A bad business, that. I don't like to think back to it.… Mind you, you should have seen the other fellow!"

The tailor laughed sympathetically and carried on pinning. The incident had enhanced their intimacy, and Montmorency began to feel confident again. As long as he and Scarper took a break from thieving for a while, they should be safe. And they would make the most of their enforced leisure. Lyons's boy had got an opera ticket for Tuesday night, and Montmorency intended to use it.

23. *La* TRAVIATA

Montmorency's cab clattered towards Covent Garden as the cool sunlight of the early May day began to give way to evening. The shops were closed and the streets were quiet, until, as they turned from the Strand into Bow Street, they hit a traffic jam of carriages dropping off the rest of the audience. Montmorency had left himself plenty of time, unsure of how long it would take him to find his seat, but plenty of others seemed to have had the same idea. He decided to get out and walk the short distance to the opera house. He stayed well to the side of the road and stepped carefully. The press of horses had deposited piles of dung here and there, and as carriage doors swung open he had to take care not to be hit, or have his new hat knocked into the dusty road. Two familiar figures were leaning against a wall, shouting saucy comments to the crowd. He was about to smile at Mrs. Evans and Vi when he remembered who he was. Vi gave him a sideways grin, with a pout and a flick of her curls, but the "Hello, darling" wasn't a gesture of recognition. It was as meaningless as the "All right, dearie?" that greeted the next man, dressed like him, in the uniform of the rich on a night out.

He followed the others into the grand foyer of the theater, slipping his hand into his pocket time and again to check that he hadn't forgotten or lost his ticket. He had memorized the number on it before he'd left the Marimion: Balcony Stalls B36. He looked for a sign to direct him to his seat. All around, couples were chatting and laughing. A line of men pressed against the bar, waving money at harassed barmen, who were pouring out champagne as fast as they could manage without filling the glasses with nothing but bubbles. Around him, the scent of a dozen different ladies' perfumes mingled and made him feel quite uncomfortable. He was nervous. He didn't know what to do. He decided to copy the only unattached man he could see: a short, stout fellow whose clothes, though high quality, were well-worn, with a generous sprinkling of dandruff on the shoulders. He obviously knew his way about. Montmorency followed him over to a kiosk in the corner, where he watched him buy a program and got one for himself. Then they shuffled off to the grand staircase opposite, where two footmen stood at either side. Montmorency's guide flashed his ticket and received a polite "Good evening, sir" from the attendant. He was obviously a regular. Montmorency held out his ticket, pointing to the number, and raising his eyebrows in an appeal for help. Just as politely, but with significantly less warmth, the footman pointed up the steps. "Up these steps, then the next."

Montmorency had to make his way through another larger bar when he reached the first level. There were huge mirrors everywhere. Once or twice he saw someone striding purposefully towards him, only to realize that it was himself, reflected, coming the other way. What appeared to be a long hall, with a series of grand chandeliers disappearing into the far distance, was in fact one room, the reflection bounced over and over again between two mirrors at either end. Eventually, he found his way into the auditorium, and after squinting at the numbers and letters marked on tiny signs, reached what he believed to be his seat. He was the first to arrive in his row, and he sat uneasily, worried that someone else might come to claim the place. For what was supposed to be an entertainment, this was pretty nerve-racking. He collapsed his hat, slid it under his seat, and waited.

People gradually settled around him. On one side was a vast old gentleman who cleared his throat with a grating rasp every few seconds. From the other, the heavy satin skirt of a grand dress billowed over onto his seat, and he could hear the creak of a corset every time the woman moved. Both his neighbors were turned away from him, in animated conversation with their companions. He felt very alone. He was hot. It was too dark to read the program and, anyway, it was difficult for him to move his arms without knocking the people on either side. In front of him sat an elegant woman with a long, slender neck. Little wisps of downy hair escaped from an elaborate coiffure on top of her head. Montmorency wondered how he would be able to see the stage with that in the way, but then he noticed the clasp on the back of her necklace. The little clip was gold, set with tiny pearls. If that was what it was like at the back, how exquisite mustthe front view be? For several minutes he was preoccpied with trying to catch a glimpse of it, to make an estimate of its worth. He failed, but in his fidgeting discovered a position that would give him a full view of the opera when it began.

The giant red velvet curtains were closed over the stage, but there was activity in the orchestra pit as musicians arrived and assembled their instruments. Random notes and funny little slides and half phrases burst out and then stopped. It didn't sound very musical.

If this is what opera's like, thought Montmorency, *I don't know how I'm going to make it through the evening.* He realized that he was trapped. There was no way he could leave without disturbing a line of people, each of whom was wedged into their seat by the bulk of their clothes. His knees were hard up against the seat in front. He could feel the beginnings of a cramp in one calf and an unbearable urge to stretch out his legs. He knew from the comings and goings at Scarper's house that the performance would last about three hours. And he realized that unless he was prepared to face the embarrassment of making half a row of people stand up to let him out, he would just have to put up with it.

The racket from the orchestra suddenly stopped, and a bald man dressed just like one of the audience made his way out from under the stage to the rostrum at the front. There was applause. He turned towards the seats and bowed briefly. Then, picking up a stick, he faced the musicians and lifted his arms. There was a hush, and then the most exquisite sound Montmorency had ever heard.

First the violins set up a note that was little more than a vibration. It swelled gradually into a tune, pulling faster and then dripping into a dance beat overlaid with sweeps of sadness and trips of joy. Cellos and double basses swept in with a melancholy grandeur and flourishes of menace, danced again, and then slowed and died back into a gentle sigh. Montmorency was about to clap when, with an urgent pulsing from the strings, the curtain opened and a brilliant world of dance and laughter was revealed in an explosion of light. A grand party was in progress. Cymbals clashed and the singing began. He was hooked.

Montmorency had been quite unprepared for the festival of music, singing, and dancing he found before him. Unprepared, too, for the many confusions. He couldn't make out a word anyone was singing, and soon deduced that they weren't singing in English. He wasn't entirely sure what was going on, or who everyone was, but he got the idea that the two people who sang most were in love, then separated, then back together again, and that the woman was very ill. He welcomed the two intervals that let him stretch his legs and explore the bar, but each time he longed to get back to the story and the music, and (except for a rather boring bit in the middle when an old man came on and sang for a long time about he knew not what) he quite forgot how squashed he was and how long he had been sitting still. At the end, as the star sang lustily from her sickbed, he found himself praying that she would survive. When the curtain fell as she collapsed onto her pillow and her lover sank to his knees in despair, the scene swam through his tears, and he joined the rest of the audience in rapturous applause. He wiped his eyes with what he thought was his handkerchief. It was a flounce from his neighbor's dress. She looked at him in alarm, then smiled and raised it to her own moist eyes. Together they cheered the performers as they stepped forward to bow to the crowd. His happiness was complete.

24. $\mathcal{F}$LUSHED

OUT?

The trip to the opera was the highlight of Montmorency's little holiday, but he knew he should not risk going out in public too often. For the rest of the time he lived quietly at the Marimion, eating, resting, and reading. He bought a book about opera, and found out exactly what had been going on in *La Traviata*. He visited the museums and art galleries, with only half an eye on the possibilities of theft. It was in many ways the life of comfort he had dreamed of for so long, but from time to time he tired of the calm and seclusion. Scarper got restless, too, and for now, mingling with others was easier as Scarper than as Montmorency. After the rich food of the Marimion he could find himself longing for bread and cheese and beer. Sometimes he changed into Scarper's clothes and took himself off to the pubs and eating houses where the porters from Covent Garden market had their breakfast. Later in the day he made for the places where the flushers took their breaks. He heard their stories of life in the tunnels, collected their trade secrets, and enjoyed their gossip about families, neighbors, and sports. The voice and habits he needed to blend in with his surroundings still came naturally, even if the manners of people he understood down to the last gesture sometimes revolted him now. Having concentrated so hard on refining his own behavior and tastes, he felt a touch of contempt for a man who spat on the pavement in front of him, and disdain for a girl picking the pockets of mourners leaving a church.

But he still had to be careful. He listened more than he spoke. He made nodding acquaintances, but no friends, and when he felt the regulars of one pub were getting to know him too well, he moved on to another. He didn't take sides in disputes. He kept out of fights. But at the same time he avoided being too aloof, which would attract attention. As Montmorency, he had become used to taking care over even the smallest detail so that no one would suspect he was a fraud. With time, he was having to watch himself as Scarper, too. Once, as he sat drinking by the fire in a dingy inn, a couple of the flushers moved towards him to share the warmth and a game of cards. He noticed how clean his hands looked against the filth of the glass. Furtively, he dug his fingernails into the sooty brickwork, just in time.

"It was really strange," said one of the flushers to his companion. "Nice bits of stuff. Boots, a lamp, a sack, just hanging there on the ladder."

Scarper was gripped by panic. The flushers had found his kit.

"No doubt about it," said the other sewer man. "You've got a private dredger."

Scarper was fighting to stay calm now, trying to look uninterested, then worrying that a normal person would be intrigued and try to join in. He wondered if he should ask a question, and opened his mouth, but it was too dry to force out more than a squeak. He must have been looking bewildered. One of the men decided to fill him in on the conversation.

"We work down the drains, see. If you can stand the stench there's all sorts of things to be found. Money, clothes, everything. We reckon someone's been down there single-handed."

"Madness. It's a dangerous place."

"If you fall in, you can get stuck in that sludge...."

"And with no one to pull you out ..."

"And the stink and the filth and the diseases ..."

"They're lucky we're willing to do it for the money we get...."

"So he's mad to do it for nothing...."

Scarper knew he had to join in the exchanges, agonized by the thought that he might give something away.

"So why would he do it?" he asked. Hoping it would sound an innocent enough question, while showing him whether they were on to his game.

"Well, it's the pickings, see...."

"The pickings, the losings, the droppings ..."

They adopted the patronizing tone of experts.

"Where do you think things go when you lose them?"

"When you drop something in the street ..."

"When you sling something out ..."

"Where do you think it ends up?"

"Down the drain, see."

"And that's where we come in. If we didn't clean it up the whole world would be awash with filth...."

"Awash with filth ..."

"And this poor soul thinks it's worth going down to fish the stuff out."

"Must be desperate ..."

"And stupid."

Scarper was relieved. They didn't seem to suspect him, but he thought he'd risk another question. "So what are you going to do?"

"Do?"

"About the things you found?"

"Oh, we'll keep them...."

"I've got the lamp. Always does to have a spare ..."

"And the foreman's got the boots. They're good ones. Nice and dry inside ..."

"And that nutcase doesn't know it, but we're doing him a favor ..."

"It's dangerous down there...."

"And there's no real money in the drains...."

"If there was, do you think we'd still be doing the job?"

"I tell you, if there was money in it, we'd cash in and get out."

"Yes," said Scarper, "I bet you would." He was thinking of how he would be returning, and how he would have to get some new gear together when the time came. But with the flushers on the lookout for intruders into their secret world, he'd have to lie low a while longer.

One of the flushers was shuffling the cards. This time he dealt three hands, and Scarper stayed with them, listening to their chatter for the rest of the afternoon.

He walked back through Covent Garden. He had to pay the rent and knew he should put in enough appearances to stop Mrs. Evans letting out his room to someone else. He bounded up the stairs humming a tune from *La Traviata*. Door number four opened, and Albert, the stagehand, put his head out. He seemed surprised to see Scarper.

"Oh, sorry, I thought it was Charlie, what with that tune. It's from *Traviata*, you know."

"Really? What's that then?" said Scarper, thinking on his feet, and the stagehand gave him a rather more entertaining account of the opera than Montmorency had found in his book at the Marimion.

"It's on tonight, you know. I wouldn't fancy being in the audience, though. Not with the weather this hot. That place gets like an oven. Mind you, on a night like this they leave the back doors open. If you go past the flower market you can hear the whole thing."

Scarper tried not to look excited, but once he had paid off Mrs. Evans, he made his way to the back of the opera house, and in the shadow cast by its enormous walls he sat and waited for the thrill of hearing the overture again.

It was there that he saw the musicians arriving with their instruments and dashing over to the pub in the intervals. There that he heard the thumps and squeaks of the scenery moving around the stage. There that he was transported once again into the magical world of Italian sound. And there that he found the discarded newspaper that brought him news of Freakshow. The pathetic old crook had now been labeled "The Hopping Horror" by the press. His trial was to begin the next day, and Montmorency was determined to go.

25. THE TRIAL

He lay awake at the Marimion well into the night, re-running the opera in his mind, and wondering whether to go to the trial as Montmorency or Scarper. In the end the fear of being recognized by someone from his prison days won over concern about being overdressed, and in the morning he strode out with his top hat and cane towards the court. Dressing up turned out to have been a good idea. After all the press attention Freakshow's arrest had attracted, there was a long line for the public gallery, but when the ushers saw Montmorency they assumed he must be one of the supposed victims come to see the thief face justice, and they made sure he got a seat. It was as cramped as the opera house, with a greater variety and strength of human smells, and the same air of theatrical excitement. As the judge entered and the prisoner was brought up from the cells, Montmorency had a faint flashback to his own trial, all those years ago, when he had been so weak and uncomprehending. But where his appearance had been routine, the judge hardly considering the evidence before sentencing him, this was a public event. There would be speeches and the newspapers were there to report them, so that by the end Freakshow would be transformed into one of the great monsters of the day.

As the accused was led up the steps to the dock there were gasps from the public gallery. Primed by the newspapers to expect a grotesque image of evil, that is what most people saw: the crutch and the wrinkled face adding to his air of menace. Montmorency saw only his old cell mate and tutor, crippled and bemused, hopelessly overwhelmed by the grandeur of the court, and quite unable to defend himself.

The case for the prosecution was simple, but formidable. Lady Bevington was dead, and her doctor confirmed that the shock of the burglary was to blame. Her son's account of the raid was dramatic. So was Sergeant Newman's. He had pressed and polished his uniform for the occasion, and delivered his evidence in a posh accent quite different from the one Montmorency had heard him use in the pub. When he had given details of the arrest, the prosecution barrister intervened.

"And tell us, Sergeant, something of the character of the defendant."

"Your honor, the defendant has been in prison several times. Indeed, he was released just over a year ago. It may please the court to note that in those few months the number of major burglaries in central London has increased dramatically. Since the arrest of the accused, that increase has been reversed."

"There have been fewer burglaries?"

"They have, as it were, gone into decline, sir."

"And you take this to be an indication that the defendant committed the other crimes?"

Freakshow muttered dissent but the judge called for silence, and weakly observed, "But he is not on trial for those crimes here."

"Indeed no, your honor," conceded the barrister, with mock humility. But the point had been made, and the jury, who seemed unsurprised by the accusation, had clearly taken everything in.

Even though there was no defense, the trial lasted for three days because the judge's summing up took longer than the evidence he was summarizing. The jury was quick with its verdict, and the judge wearily reached for the black cap he must put on when announcing a hanging. In passing sentence, he made mention of the other crimes of which Freakshow had been judged guilty by public opinion, if not by the official record.

"And it is the judgment of this court that you be taken from this court to the place in which you were detained, and from thence to a place of execution, where you will be hanged by the neck until you are dead. And may God have mercy on your soul. Take him down."

Then, with a tap of his gavel, he halfheartedly tried to silence the flurry of applause that broke out in the public gallery.

As the guards grabbed the one-legged man and turned him towards the steps, Freakshow looked up at the snarling crowd and caught Montmorency's eye. He looked desperate, then puzzled. Then he turned his head swiftly as if he didn't want to look again. Had he recognized his old cell mate? Had he, in that moment, realized who had been behind the crimes for which he was about to pay?

Montmorency felt an unfamiliar emotion. It was shame. But mixed with it was relief that the authorities had closed the files on his many thefts. He knew that if Freakshow had any suspicions, the last thing he would do was tell the police. He was sorry that Freakshow was going to die, but then the old fool had been at Lady Bevington's and Lady Bevington was dead. People should pay for their crimes, if they were caught. He felt that even more strongly when he reached for his wallet in a restaurant an hour later. It had gone. One of those rogues outside the court must have stolen it.

26. BACK TO THE SOCIETY

For a month after the trial, Montmorency continued his holiday, itching to get back down the sewers, but determined not to risk detection by the police or the flushers. On the day of Freakshow's hanging, Scarper joined the early morning crowd outside the prison, though he didn't join in the cheer that greeted the news that he was dead. For two days after that he stayed in his room at the Marimion, not settling at anything: sitting with books for half an hour without taking in a word; pacing up and down trying to get his old friend out of his mind; bathing, primping, and preening; then pacing again, unable to face the world.

On the third morning, he caught sight of a notice in *The Times* advertising a public lecture by Professor Humbley at the Scientific Society. He spent the afternoon wondering whether to take the risk of being recognized. At five o'clock, horrified by a poster in the hotel lobby announcing "A recital of popular ballads by Miss Cissie Longman," he decided to go.

In his convict days, Montmorency had always entered the Scientific Society building through a back door. The prison van would make its way along a narrow side street and draw up as close as possible to the service entrance. Two attendants would be waiting, one holding the door, the other darting out to open the carriage, so that Farcett could rush prisoner 493 into the building, still handcuffed to his guard. There had been no time to look around outside. Inside, narrow corridors cluttered with boxes, books, and mysterious scientific equipment led to a small opening at the back of the stage. There the shackles would be removed, the doctor would prepare his patient for display, and the two of them would slip to their seats to await their turn before the audience. When Marston accompanied them, he would pace angrily up and down backstage, until 493 was safely tied to him again. Other guards took the opportunity to sneak out for a snack at the local pub.

So it was a shock for Montmorency to discover the elegant surroundings of the front entrance. He had walked there from the Marimion, past some of the grandest private homes in London. There seemed to be building sites everywhere, as rich merchants and industrialists competed to put up more impressive homes than their neighbors'. Great institutional buildings were being constructed, too, and most of these were decorated with pillars, moldings, and fancy brickwork. Even a small maternity hospital had been given wide marble steps up to its vast double doors, and stained-glass windows depicting scenes from an idyllic childhood. Everything about the new buildings was large. The rooms were big, the ceilings were high, so that even houses with the same number of floors as older dwellings towered over them.

The Scientific Society, built more than a hundred years earlier, had, in its day, been considered a graceful building. Now its plain brick front and symmetrical windows looked almost drab against the riot of stone and ceramics on either side. Inside, though, the atmosphere was solid and academic rather than out of style. Almost the entire construction was wooden, so that it was like being on board a ship. The street doors opened into a broad antechamber. From floor to ceiling, the wall was lined with dark oak, divided into squares like a chocolate bar. The lower ones were bare, but up at eye level, every third panel housed a portrait of a great scientist. They ranged from fanciful guesses at what ancient figures like Archimedes or Galileo might have looked like, to images of long-dead men like William Harvey, who had described the circulation of the blood, and Sir Christopher Wren, who, as well as rebuilding London after the Great Fire of 1666, had been one of the foremost scientific thinkers of his day. The newer portraits included some faces Montmorency recognized from his visits with Doctor Farcett. The latest of all was of Sir Joseph Bazalgette himself, looking exactly as he had on the night he had unwittingly changed Montmorency's life.

Above the portraits, large gas lamps brought a warm glow out of the wood. The Society had been one of the first buildings in London to install gas lighting. Now its organizing committee was engaged in a protracted debate about whether to lead the way into the electric age.

At the far corners of the antechamber, two spiral staircases rose up to a gallery. Their banisters were carved with delicate designs, quite out of keeping with the more flamboyant modern style. At the top, doors led ahead into the lecture theater itself, where curved rows of benches stepped downward toward the stage. The audience for the evening had begun to gather, small groups chatting, occasionally greeting a newcomer as he or she entered from the stairs. Montmorency sat high up at the back, observing, listening, relieved that so far there were no familiar faces. He wondered if the Society's members kept clear of these "public" lectures, not wanting to mix with their intellectual inferiors. The stage had been set simply. Just a chair, a lectern, and a small table with a flagon of water and a glass. Professor Humbley was going to talk about "Developments in European Philosophy." There wouldn't be any call for the porters tonight. No strange beasts or vegetables to pass around. No prisoner 493, either, though from his perch, Montmorency could see his old chair tucked away in the distance.

"Ladies and gentlemen. We are delighted that you have visited us this evening for what I am sure will be a fascinating talk...."

Forbes Bailey-MacDonald, the diligent but rather boring secretary of the Society, was enjoying his task of introducing Professor Humbley, whose glistening face beamed as he took the stage and sat down. Forbes Bailey-MacDonald took an expensive-looking fob watch from the pocket of his waistcoat and glanced at the time, as if to ensure that his opening remarks would not overrun.

"Now, I know you haven't come to see me...." (Polite titters.) "So I won't delay the proceedings except to say that we are most extremely privileged to have with us tonight a man who needs no introduction to anyone with an interest in the great thinkers of our time...."

There was an embarrassed giggle from Humbley, who was about to rise to speak when it became clear that Bailey-MacDonald had more to say. Perhaps he had been anxious to show off his watch, rather than to limit his own speech.

"Indeed, I was reading his work on the Athenian philosophers the other day, and it brought to mind the time when I was engaged in studies of my own on that very subject in the summer of 1866. Or was it 1867?"

He stopped, and Humbley leaned forward again, just managing to lift his bottom from the seat before Bailey-MacDonald resumed.

"Possibly '68, for I believe that Masterson's work on Plato had already been published, and I reflected on how ..."

Humbley sank back into his chair again as Bailey-MacDonald continued his private performance, and the audience began to grow restless. Montmorency felt sorry for Professor Humbley, who was exposed to the full view of the audience, trying to look composed, but feeling increasingly uncomfortable. He sat on the stage fiddling with the buttons on his jacket. He twiddled the tiny flecks of hair around his ears. He managed to stop himself picking his nose, but pinched it from time to time, or flicked at it, as if a fly was bothering him. He got rather too engaged with a small piece of food lodged between his protruding front teeth. He nibbled his nails, crossed and recrossed his legs, tapped his toes on the ground, and gazed upward, sitting on his hands and appearing to take a great interest in the hall's distinctly uninteresting ceiling. Occasionally, it seemed as if Professor Humbley had nodded off, only for him to jump abruptly, pour himself some water and drink. The jug was almost empty by the time Forbes Bailey-MacDonald drew his introduction to a close.

"And we are particularly fortunate that Professor Humbley has agreed to leave his wonderful collection of antiquities and books to visit us this evening. I can assure you that if I were the tenant of Horatio House in Nelson Place, where I have had the honor of dining with tonight's illustrious guest on numerous occasions, I should be reluctant to leave such treasures. And so, with no more ado ..." He checked his watch again without so much as a raised eyebrow. "I give you Professor Septimus Humbley, and tonight's lecture: Developments in European Philosophy."

The audience was so relieved that Bailey-MacDonald had stopped talking that Humbley received a rousing welcome. He responded with one of the squeaking, toothy giggles that had so endeared him to Montmorency in the past. The contrast with the Society's secretary could not have been greater. Bailey-MacDonald was afflicted with the knack of turning the simplest speech into an ordeal for his audience. Humbley could convey the most complex ideas with a lightness of touch that made them as palatable as gossip. He was a shy man offstage, but when he was teaching he was transformed. He had the gift of making each person in the room think they were his most important listener, drawing them into his tale and making them — at least for the duration of the lecture — as excited about the subject as he was.

Montmorency was fascinated, too, feeling a curious affection, even a slight proprietorial pride for the professor, and a great relief that Humbley was winning the audience back onto his side. But Scarper had other ideas. No matter how hard the gentleman in the neatly pressed suit and stylish cape tried to concentrate on the talk, the scruffy chancer inside him couldn't let go of the most interesting information he'd heard that night. *Horatio House, Nelson Place...full of treasures, and unattended.* So often during his break from crime Montmorency had felt the lure of the sewers. He missed the excitement of his hidden brushes with danger and the thrill of outsmarting the authorities. Once or twice he had almost cracked. He had even replaced the tools and boots found by the flushers. He was longing to try out those new boots: thigh-high waders bought at a sporting outfitter's store that counted royalty among its clients. But so far he had managed to resist Scarper's promptings to get back to work. Tonight of all nights, when his proposed victim was the kind and gentle figure who had unknowingly helped him with his plans, there was no reason to give in. And yet Scarper's voice was there again, repeating the tantalizing news: *Horatio House, Nelson Place...full of treasures, and unattended.* Within fifteen minutes, Montmorency had slipped out of the hall, gone back to the Marimion, dodged Cissie's squealing recital, and changed his clothes.

Two hours later, Scarper was tucking a leather-bound translation of Plutarch and a collection of Roman coins under the floorboards in Covent Garden. Professor Humbley, who had had to endure dinner with Forbes Bailey-MacDonald after the lecture, let himself into his house desperate for sleep. The poor man had to spend half the night with Sergeant Newman, who was quietly despairing at finding another perplexing burglary on his hands.

27. HORROR UNDERGROUND

So the holiday was over. Montmorency was back in business, and he was glad. Life was too short to stay in a hotel room forever, and even though he was increasingly troubled by unfamiliar feelings of guilt, and unease at living a life sustained by crime, he needed an income, and the only way to get it was by doing what he did best. But nothing would be the same after Freakshow's death. Montmorency had had too clear a warning of the dangers of being caught. The first few jobs after Professor Humbley's lecture were widely spaced in time and location. As the months passed and the number of raids picked up, Montmorency was determined not to establish a pattern that could reawaken the interest of the police. But the risks weren't confined to the law. He was certain of that after what happened to Scarper one cold February day.

Scarper was getting cocky. After nearly two years he felt he had mastered the sewers, and knew their moods and byways, not needing his chalk markings now. The network of drains was his to use as he wanted. What was more, he was no longer desperate for cash. From the daily burglaries of his peak he had cut back to about three a week. If a danger arose he could afford to postpone a job.

One day, on the way to check out an art gallery in Kensington, the smell (which he normally no longer noticed) became unbearable. He'd heard the flushers in the pub talking about this. There must be a split pipe somewhere, leaking town gas into the raw sewage, making a potent and presumably explosive mix. He calmly put out his lamp and left as soon as he could. He'd never been sure about hitting the art market, anyway. But two days later, he couldn't resist the lure of a silversmith in Blackfriars.

Scarper got the idea for the raid while eavesdropping on some printers at a pub off the Strand. They had a new boy with them, who was showing off by telling them about his last job, from which he had been sacked a week before. Most of his tale was about his employer's appalling personal habits. The boy acted out the scene for his new friends, turning up his collar and grimacing like the old man crouched over his workbench.

"He'd sit in there all day, farting and burping." The boy made the appropriate noises and his companions fell about laughing. "I tell you, I thought I was going to suffocate in the stench." More noises, more laughter. "And he could hardly see so he'd have his work right up against his eyes, bending the metal and engraving the designs on lockets and stuff. And he'd just shout at me, 'More beer! More beer!' And I'd have to run around to the Swan and back in two minutes or he'd start swearing and spitting. 'You ****ing little ****! I'll have your ****s for ****s! Cough, cough, spit, spit, spit!' But still his head would be down, and he'd be working away on some delicate little ring or a necklace. Honestly, if some of those ladies knew where their jewelry came from! He was supposed to be teaching me, but all I could see was his hair and his hands, and I couldn't get near enough to watch what he was doing because of the stink."

More acting, more laughs.

"And all the time, he kept going, hardly moving at all. Just working, drinking, working, drinking. Then, about two o'clock, he'd just fall forward like this...." The boy dropped towards the table as a dead weight, his forehead hitting the wood with a loud crack. "And there he was for the afternoon, surrounded by all his silver. Out of it. Totally. It's a miracle he's never been robbed. The place is like a fortress at night. He's got safes and stuff, and keys as big as your hand. But I tell you after he's had a few in the day, you could just walk in and help yourself. Course I can't now, 'cos they'd know it was me."

"Yeah, well, let's skip work and go around for a handful!" laughed one of the men.

They all roared. But six feet away, Scarper wasn't joking as he ran through the sewer map in his mind. He knew the Swan, and reckoned he could find the silversmith from the boy's description of the area. He drank up quickly, and went home to pick up his equipment for an easy afternoon's work.

He hadn't been in the tunnel long when he heard the familiar *clang* of a manhole cover being dropped into place. *Good,* he thought, *the flushers are off for a break. I won't be disturbed.* Seconds later, the crash came again. *Clumsy ...* Then again and again, so that a violent echoing racket was set up, the sound pulsing though the tunnels and sending the rats scurrying along the brickwork. Scarper realized it must be some sort of signal from workers on the surface to a gang down below. It didn't sound like a dinner bell. Something must be up. He thought of turning around and going home, but he was halfway to Blackfriars now, and it was just as quick to go on. He took the lamp from his head and examined the flame. It was burning normally. No strange gases. He would continue.

Just as he was about to move forward, he noticed ripples on the surface of the sewage. Soon they were little waves, and a huge wind swept towards him, unbalancing him and throwing him onto his back in the sludge. His right wader started to fill with liquid, fastening him to the tunnel floor. He fought to keep his head high while kicking and wrenching his body to cast the boot away and set his leg free. Looking up, he could see great spouts of water shooting from the mouths of drains that normally only sent a trickle down the walls. He realized what must be happening, and why the sewer men had raced to get one another out.

There was a storm over London.

The water from the street foamed and spurted as it hit the flow of sewage, raising the level so that Scarper's face was only just above the surface. His second wader was almost full. He had to get the boots off, or he would be trapped, unable to breathe. He twisted and pulled his body against the relentless sucking of the sludge and the strengthening tug of the water, as its growing volume sped the flow ever onward to the east. At last his legs were free, but now he could not stand. The raging pressure buffeted him along, slapping him against the walls time and time again. Rubbish that had sat stuck in the slurry for months was up and on the move. Debris of all sorts slammed against him, tearing at his skin. His sleeve caught on a ladder and was ripped away as his body was carried still farther, faster and faster in the darkness and noise. The tunnel seemed endless, then he realized that the black space in front of him had a hardness and solidity about it. He was about to be crushed against a vast metal wall. He could do nothing except try to find some air at the top of the torrent.

Then the roar of the water was joined by an iron squealing and a mighty groan as the wall appeared to split in two across the middle, swinging away and letting in a jet of blinding light. Scarper knew he must be dying. He sank below the waves, then found himself propelled through the air on a tube of foam. The dank atmosphere of the tunnel was replaced by a rush of cold air, followed by the icy suction of deep water. The force of the flood had opened the storm relief gate. The sewer had overflowed into the Thames and taken him with it.

Swooping between consciousness and oblivion, he could see nothing, and couldn't tell which way was up or down. He flapped and kicked until his face broke the surface just as his lungs seemed about to explode. A rope tethering a barge came within reach of his hand. He held on, shivering and crying in the rain.

The river was deserted. The boatmen had noticed the darkening skies long ago, as Scarper had set off down his manhole without a thought for the weather aboveground. By the time the water had grown dangerously rough, their boats were safely moored and they were sheltering somewhere warm, sharing stories of storms and disasters long past. Scarper had no sense of how long he had been in the water. In a moment of reason, he had twisted the rope around and around his arm, so that even the pull of the tide could not untangle him, then his brain shut off and he drifted, bumping against the side of the barge, not thinking or feeling anything, numbed by the cold and without the strength even to fight for life. He didn't notice as the rain stopped and the river grew calmer. He didn't hear as the bargeman, checking on his craft after the deluge, shouted to his mate.

"Come here with that hook. There's something tangled in the line."

A boy, who had been bailing out water from inside the boat, lazily made his way to the stern, then froze as he realized that the limp mess hanging from the side was a human body. The bargeman grabbed the hook, and the two of them hauled Scarper from the water and tried, with little hope, to coax some breath from his body.

28. STRUGGLING HOME

Hours later, thanks to the rivermen's kindness and strength, Scarper was back in his room. He was bruised, battered, cut, but most of all exhausted, and he slept right through the following day. When he woke he knew he had to get back to the Marimion, not just for its comforts and care, but because questions would be asked if Montmorency was away for too long.

He dressed, slowly, painfully, unable to button his shirt or tie his boots. Retrieving the Marimion key from its hiding place under the floor, he picked up enough money from his store of treasure to pay for a cab ride to Hyde Park. He got out well away from the hotel. The driver was bound to remember him in his bedraggled state, and he didn't want to leave a trail. He lurked by the Marimion's trash cans until he was sure the back entrance was clear, got himself upstairs, and struggled with the lock. Montmorency's clothes were even more unmanageable than usual, and when he had changed into them the image he saw in the huge mirrors was almost unrecognizable in its disarray. There was a frantic knocking at the door, and Longman's concerned voice.

"Mr. Montmorency, are you in there?"

Montmorency knew he had to respond. He tried to shout a reassuring reply, but no voice would come. He shuffled to the door and opened it the tiniest crack.

The manager recoiled at the sight of the injured man. "What on earth has happened to you? We've been so worried...."

Montmorency gave the first reply that came into his head, but it was inspired. "We have been attacked."

Longman was all concern. He helped Montmorency to the bed, asking — with little success — for the details of the incident. He wanted to send for the police, but Montmorency insisted there was no point. It had been dark. He and Scarper had been hit from behind, and had seen nothing of the thugs who had jumped them. Longman was also for fetching a doctor. Montmorency was horrified. Suppose they got Farcett, or any other of the Scientific Society medics, who might not recognize his face, but would certainly know him by his ancient scars?

"Scarper has already gone for one," he said. (This explained the servant's absence, too.) "Please, leave me alone. I need to sleep."

"But perhaps a little food and some brandy?" suggested Longman, and Montmorency realized that he had not eaten since before the storm. As Longman left to arrange for a tray to be sent up, Montmorency flopped back onto the bed to plan out how to play the next few days.

As he expected, the main problem was Cissie. She had kept out of Montmorency's way since the incident with Scarper backstairs, but the opportunity to tend her injured hero was too good to miss. At first, Montmorency answered her timid knocks and piping inquiries with short reassurances that he was getting better and needed to be left alone. But he did need some practical help, and Cissie was more than willing to be sent on errands for dressings, liniments, and other medical items. She took to bringing them back wearing a sort of nurse's apron, at first stiffly starched and gleaming, but after a while somewhat spattered with food. She was determined to get into the room to see the patient, and complained about having to leave the supplies on the floor outside, claiming it was "unhygienic." Montmorency pulled on Scarper's shirt and opened the door just enough to grab them from her with a scowl that sent her scurrying down the stairs. But she was back, tapping and squeaking again before long.

Montmorency realized that she was bound to get a better look sometime, and that he would have to take precautions against her noticing that his and Scarper's injuries were identical. He looked in the mirror. There was a deep graze over the left eye. He would cover it with a large bandage around his head. If he made it like a hat, he could pull it on and off, leaving poor Scarper to suffer his wound uncovered. In exchange, Scarper could have a bandage all up one arm (loose enough to slip off like a glove), and Montmorency could have a sling. He had difficulty constructing this last prop, and resorted to opening the door a little to ask Cissie to tie it behind his neck for him.

"Scarper's out," he told her. "He'd be furious if he knew I'd asked you to help me."

She liked that. Not quite a proposal, but she liked it.

29. $\mathscr{I}$NVALIDS

For a fortnight after the storm, Montmorency was confined to his room, treating his own injuries with a professional skill learned in his time as Robert Farcett's living exhibit. As a prisoner he had silently ridiculed the doctor's obsession with cleanliness: his nagging of the staff about "sepsis," "asepsis," and "antisepsis." (Montmorency had told one nurse that he had an Auntie Sepsis in Camberwell, but she didn't get the joke.) Now, though, he was careful to be clean. The flushers loved frightening other drinkers in the pub with accounts of terrible deaths from the special diseases of their underground trade. The worst started with a headache and left you dead within a day. When Montmorency woke in the middle of the night he imagined himself in the grip of that malady, or the mystery germ that attacked your eyeballs and left you blind. So when he got up, he went straight for a soak in the bath, then applied more creams and lotions to his healing body, and returned to bed. He couldn't always settle down. His mind ran on to the future. Would he ever have the courage or the physical strength to return to the sewers? How long could he continue to operate in that world? Was there no other way of achieving the comforts he had grown to love so much? Certainly not if he didn't get better. He needed rest. He pulled the covers over his head and tried to sleep.

But he couldn't stay there all day. Scarper had to be accounted for in the backstairs world, and he would have to put in some appearances there. The attack on him and his master had brought them the attention they had worked so hard to avoid and he knew that that interest could turn to suspicion if it was not fed with some facts. So a couple of times a day, Montmorency's silk pajamas had to be removed, and Scarper's rough clothes painfully pulled on. He took to visiting the kitchen just before mealtimes, saying he had come to get a plate of dinner for his master but, in fact, taking advantage of the frenzy of activity so that no one would take too much notice of him. He built on the story Montmorency had concocted for Mr. Longman, setting the drama in an alley between the opera house and Covent Garden market, and describing how a gang had sneaked up behind them, stealing Montmorency's watch, money, and walking stick, and threatening Scarper with a knife. The kitchen maids were fascinated by his bravery. Some of the porters insisted that they would have done more to defend themselves. At a safe distance, Cissie listened in, despising Scarper for his failure to protect his master.

As Montmorency's bruises turned from black to blue, from blue to brown, and from brown to yellow, he let himself believe that he had not contracted some horrible sewer disease, and eased up on the painstaking disinfection of his wounds. Doctor Farcett's other obsession had been movement. Injured limbs must be exercised. Muscle tone must be restored. Montmorency didn't fancy the hard labor of the prison model, but he did decide to go for walks in the park to bring back his strength.

From his room, on days when the smoke from London's chimneys had not curdled the fog into smog, he had a clear view of the enormous green space that was one of the town's lungs. If he went onto the balcony, he could look down on the chaotic traffic: an undisciplined sprawl of horses, carriages, and pedestrians, and then across the road to the calm of the park. In the early morning, shop workers, and even some of the Marimion's own staff could be seen hurrying along the paths, anxious to get to work, and hardly noticing their surroundings at all. Later, children would play with balls or hoops, and wealthier adults walked at a more leisurely pace. He observed how the men conducted themselves: how they wore their clothes, held their gloves, and used their canes. He saw them stop, bow forward slightly, and mechanically lift their hats when they met an acquaintance coming the other way. Occasionally, they would steer a female companion with a light touch on the elbow, but apart from some stolen kisses that the participants thought they were taking in secret, there were few signs of obvious affection, more a sense of gentle style on display. At night, the dark expanse was a more menacing place. More than once, Montmorency had heard a scream in the distance, but however hard he looked, he couldn't detect the source or the cause.

Until recently, Montmorency had not ventured far into the park himself. He'd used it as a shortcut from time to time, and had paused for a while watching people letting off steam at Speaker's Corner, where anyone could stand on a soapbox and say what they liked without fear of being moved on by the police. One Sunday a small, pinched little man with a narrow mustache, tight trousers, and impressively clean boots was blasting off about the need for a tougher regime in prisons. He claimed convicts were living lives of indulgence and luxury.

"The law-abiding citizen is forced to pay for these monsters, these fiends, to inhabit what are tantamount to grand hotels, with a staff of hundreds waiting upon them like servants! And while we pour our money into these palaces, there are more and more thieves on the streets trying to rob us! And no wonder, I say. Today's criminals aren't frightened of being caught! The villains can't wait to get inside! I say bring back the rack. Hanging is too good for them!"

Montmorency had to stop himself hitting back with his own inside knowledge. He just gave a grunt of disapproval that could be interpreted either way, and moved on.

Now that he needed the exercise, he took to walking briskly into the heart of the gardens. He enjoyed the air, the plants, and watching uniformed nannies with their wonderful prams. Inevitably, though, there was also Cissie. He suspected that she watched from a high perch at the hotel waiting to spot him and swoop. Suddenly, she would be there at his side, prattling away about the lives and loves of the rich and famous people who had stayed at the Marimion or were promenading in the park. At first, his tactic was to walk faster in the hope of leaving her behind, but she just ran along panting and, worse still, grabbed on to his arm snorting as she got her breath back. He removed the hand with a polite gesture indicating his injury, but he couldn't shake her off completely and decided instead to make use of her encyclopedic knowledge of London society, acquired from a dedicated study of scandal sheets and magazines.

So he slowed down, he listened and stored the information. It was a relief that once she got going, she was incapable of maintaining the annoying lisp she usually adopted just for him. Occasionally (though it was rarely necessary), he asked a question. He never revealed anything about himself and, as long as he kept her talking, Cissie didn't have time to ask. Having cheated death, he now wanted to have some fun, and he determined that as soon as he was well enough he would dive into the delights of the dances, drinking, gambling, and vice of which she spoke with such relish. His introduction to that world came sooner than he had intended.

30. A DRAMA

One afternoon he was weaving his way through the traffic on his way back to the hotel, with Cissie jabbering at his heels. They were about halfway across the road when an elderly horse pulling a cab suddenly shied alongside him, waving its hooves in the air and letting out a searing nasal scream. Frightened that he would be kicked and hurt yet again, Montmorency instinctively grabbed the reins. The horse gave a gargling splutter and collapsed, dead, on the spot. Montmorency expected trouble. He expected the driver to blame him for the death of his horse and to demand compensation. He certainly didn't expect to be hailed as a hero, which he suddenly was, on all sides.

The traffic came to a standstill around the sorry scene, and people ran from the sidewalks and the park to see what was going on. Cissie was convinced that Montmorency had saved her life (nothing had been farther from his mind) and instantly started describing the incident to the gathering crowd. Even though many of them had seen it all themselves, they came to believe, with her, that the beast had galloped out of control all the way from Marble Arch, and that Montmorency had risked injury or death by intervening on her behalf.

But Cissie was outdone in her gushing praise by the passenger in the cab. It took him a while to get out, for he was large in all directions — though the first part of his body to emerge was a tiny foot, clad in a fashionably tight and shiny shoe. The rest of his clothes were equally up to date. In fact, Montmorency, with his new interest in gentlemen's clothing, was able to identify them as the work of one of London's most expensive tailors. When the stranger finally stood up by the side of the road, he looked like a wobbly-man toy, narrow at the bottom, wide in the middle, and narrow again at the top, for he had little hair above his ears — though his bushy beard more than made up for that. When he put on his hat, which had been rather crumpled in the commotion, he looked more normal — even, thought Cissie, quite handsome, but she still found it hard to believe that those little feet could support so large a man.

He held out his hand to Montmorency. "George Fox-Selwyn."

"It's Lord George Fox-Selwyn," Cissie whispered excitedly. "Son of the Marquess of—"

"Montmorency," interrupted the hero, embarrassed by her audible enthusiasm. "I'm at the Marimion. Perhaps you should come in to get your breath back."

"Can't thank you enough, old boy." Fox-Selwyn now had Montmorency by the arm, recognizing a man of his own class when he saw one. "I think it's no exaggeration to say that you have saved my life."

The two of them made their way up the steps for a brandy while Cissie stayed outside, swapping gossip about the Fox-Selwyns with a woman from the crowd, and the cabman said a sad farewell to his old horse, who, he insisted with a sob, had "had a good life."

After a while, a policeman arrived, and slowly untangled the traffic. Some of the crowd stayed to watch the cab and the dead horse being dragged to the edge of the park by a gang of workmen from a building site. The driver stayed with his horse as dusk fell, occasionally giving its lifeless body an affectionate pat. Eventually, a battered cart arrived, and a menacing character in a brown overall started negotiating with the miserable cabbie. Money changed hands, and the old horse was secured with ropes and hauled up a ramp and into the cart, to be taken away and rendered down to hide, grease, and glue.

Montmorency and Fox-Selwyn watched all this from the comfort of the Marimion bar. When the horse was taken away, Montmorency excused himself for a moment and crossed the road under cover of darkness to give the cabbie some money towards a new one. He surprised himself with the gesture. Only a few weeks earlier his mind would have been preoccupied with how to pick Fox-Selwyn's pocket. Scarper must have been asleep that night.

When Montmorency said good-bye to Fox-Selwyn on the front steps hours later, it was only after accepting an invitation to visit his new friend at his club — Bargles — not far from Trafalgar Square, on the other side of the park.

31. $\mathcal{F}$ox-selwyn
AND THE DOCTOR

Stepping out of bed the next morning, Lord George Fox-Selwyn discovered that he couldn't put any weight on his left foot without a pain shooting up into his leg. Something had been damaged in the accident. His head didn't feel too brilliant, either, but that was probably due to the brandy at the Marimion. He called in Chivers, his valet, and asked his opinion on the injury.

"I'd see a doctor, sir, if I were you. You should never take chances with feet, sir. Everything else depends upon them."

"Especially if I'm going to Lady Ellingham's ball, eh? Send over to old Barnes and get him to come and have a look, will you?"

"Sir, you may remember that Doctor Barnes was himself unwell when we last inquired after him."

"That was long ago, he must be better by now. He's a doctor, isn't he? He should know what medicine to take."

"He is no longer unwell, sir."

"Then, fetch him."

"He is dead, sir."

"Well, that's not much of a recommendation. What am I supposed to do about this foot?"

"With respect, sir, I have heard that several of doctor Barnes's patients are now being attended by a Doctor Farcett. He's rather younger, but fast making a name for himself."

"Well, get him then. But he'll have to be here before noon. I'm having lunch at the club."

Robert Farcett was indeed thriving. His list of patients had grown considerably since old Barnes had succumbed to the chest disease that had made him famous for spluttering over even the most refined of his clients. They had been delighted with the cleaner manners and more effective treatments of his young colleague, and word of his talents was spreading in society. He was at last beginning to make some money out of his work, but not enough yet to allow him to ignore Fox-Selwyn's cry for help, even though he had several other invalids to visit that day. As they entered Fox-Selwyn's house in Knightsbridge, Chivers and the doctor could hear his lordship hopping about, attempting to dress himself for lunch. Fox-Selwyn collapsed back onto his bed.

"At last! I was wondering where on earth you were. Damned painful, this! My nanny always said injuries were worse on the second day."

"She was right," said Farcett. "It's the buildup of bruising and fluid in the tissues around the wound."

Fox-Selwyn was impressed and raised his eyebrows appreciatively, signaling to Chivers his approval of the new man. Doctor Barnes had never shown any interest in the details of illness, let alone any actual knowledge.

"Took me half an hour to get this sock on, and now I suppose you're going to make me take it off!"

"I'm afraid so," said Doctor Farcett sympathetically. "I need to have a proper look at the wound." (More raised eyebrows.) "How exactly did it happen?"

Farcett had been wanting simply to find out whether the foot had been twisted, crushed, or knocked. Instead he was treated to a full (rather overfull) account of the accident. By the time Fox-Selwyn had finished, the doctor had determined the need for firm strapping and some painkillers.

"Give me something powerful," said Fox-Selwyn, patting his vast stomach. "It will take a lot to get through here down to that foot."

"Well, I have got some drugs with me, but I do keep something a little stronger locked up at home. Perhaps I could just pop back and get it...." The ornate clock on the mantelpiece chimed twelve dainty chimes. "Though I am expecting a patient there very shortly, and it might be a while before I can return."

"And I've got to get off to my club," said Fox-Selwyn, "I'm lunching with the man who rescued me yesterday. Tell you what. Why don't I come with you? We can pick up the pills, and then I'll take the cab back into town. What do you think? Eh?"

Farcett knew he had no option but to agree if he was to keep this lucrative patient on his books, and within half an hour they were pulling up outside the doctor's house. He had been hoping Fox-Selwyn would stay in the cab, but he hobbled out and, chatting all the way, followed him into the chaotic study. As Farcett unlocked his medicine chest, Fox-Selwyn blathered on, picking books off the shelves and leafing through them, and commenting on the graphic illustrations of illnesses and injuries on the walls. Finally, he noticed the detailed depiction of prisoner 493, his injuries annotated up the side, with the dates and details of each operation, and the site of each wound and scar clearly marked.

"What's this, then? Some sort of surgical instruction chart?"

"It's one of my patients, actually."

"What, you did all that to him? It's a wonder he's still alive."

"Oh, he is. Or at least, I hope he is. He nearly died — more than once — but we got there in the end." And Farcett told Fox-Selwyn the story of prisoner 493. "I had hoped I could continue to treat him after his release, but he never got in touch. I often wonder what has become of him."

"Returned to a life of crime, I suppose."

"Probably. But I always thought he might make rather more of himself. I certainly can't imagine him risking a return to prison. He was in with that one-legged man they hanged a while back, the one who killed Lady Bevington."

"Ah, 'The Hopping Horror'!"

"They shared a cell. I wouldn't have believed he was a murderer, either. Perhaps I'm just a bad judge of character."

"Well, as long as you're a good judge of painkillers. I think I'll have a couple of these right away." Fox-Selwyn helped himself to some brandy from a decanter on the sideboard to wash them down.

"I think one at a time is enough, and perhaps better with some water...." Farcett knew it was hopeless to protest. But even so, he added, "And they should ideally be taken with food."

"Well, then, I'd better get off to lunch. You know where to send the bill."

As Fox-Selwyn opened the door, a ragged woman could be seen, carrying a sick child up the drive.

"And my next patient's here," said Farcett, slightly embarrassed at being caught out with one of his charity cases.

Fox-Selwyn was intrigued. There was obviously more to this man than there had been to Doctor Barnes.

"Thank you. I feel better already," he called as he limped speedily off to the cab. "I hope we don't have cause to meet again, but I shall be delighted if we do."

"Thank you, my lord," said Farcett, wondering whether it was the pills, the brandy, or the thought of lunch that had brought on Fox-Selwyn's recovery.

32. BARGLES CLUB

Bargles was a dark, flat-fronted building, as restrained on the outside as the Marimion was showy. The entrance, a small door down half a dozen narrow steps, was unmarked, to avoid public attention. The club was strictly for members and their guests. It was impossible to enter without being scrutinized by an attendant in a little kiosk on one side of the porch. The cabbie had known the address, but Montmorency found it hard to believe he was in the right place until he saw Fox-Selwyn burst through onto the pavement to greet him.

"He's with me, Sam!" he shouted to the porter, as Montmorency handed in his hat and cloak.

"We'll be in Smokes if anybody wants me."

"Very good, my lord."

"Smokes," as Montmorency guessed, turned out to be the smoking room. Later, he was to discover the dining rooms: "Big Eats" (referred to by the more boyish members as "Eats Major") and "Little Eats" ("Eats Minor"). There were also bars: "Big Drinks" and "Little Drinks" (each with its Latin tag: "Drinks Major," "Drinks Minor"); "Private Drinks" (also known as "Plotters"); a library ("Swotters"); and a terrace ("The Parade") leading to a small garden ("Outers"). The washrooms and lavatories were "Wetties" and "Ploppers," respectively. On the top floor there were bedrooms, where members could stay if they were only visiting town, or at times of domestic crisis. Montmorency asked what these were called.

"Bedrooms, of course," Fox-Selwyn replied, completely mystified by the question.

In Smokes, Drinks, and Eats, Fox-Selwyn summoned and dispatched waiters to bring the pair (and a stream of other men who joined them) sustenance to get them through the afternoon and into the evening. Montmorency was increasingly bemused. Every servant seemed to be called Sam. He knew he'd had a lot to drink but he was sure it wasn't the same man every time. His conviction was confirmed when Fox-Selwyn memorably shouted, "Sam, can you tell Sam that we'll be in to Plotters later for a brandy, and then get Sam to call us a cab."

Montmorency hardly needed to ask. All the servants were known as Sam. It made things easier for the members of Bargles (the cream of the British empire). Otherwise they might have had to trouble themselves with thinking.

By the end of that first night, Montmorency had met twenty or more of Fox-Selwyn's friends, each in turn treated to a more dramatic account of Montmorency and the runaway horse. By the end of the week, after daily visits, the Sams would greet him enthusiastically, and even engage in polite chitchat. Unbeknownst to Montmorency, the cloakroom attendant had assigned him his own special peg. After a fortnight of mixing with the members of the club he was even acquiring a nickname, though it was not clear yet whether this would settle as Monty, Monto, or Monters.

No one asked him much about himself. When they did, he found the best tactic was to turn the conversation around and ask about the questioner. They all seemed to prefer talking about themselves. Even so, a past and a background were being created for him. Fox-Selwyn so often referred to Montmorency as "my savior" that his Christian name was taken to be Xavier, which only served to heighten the air of exotic mystery that surrounded him. When asked about the origin of his surname, he simply said, "French, way back," leaving others to fill in the picture of a noble family ousted from their homeland by revolution. The subject having shifted to "abroad," Fox-Selwyn could then be relied upon to chip in with his own stories of foreign travel and dramatic adventures, which were both interesting and (judging by their consistency) true.

Through the spring and summer, Montmorency and Fox-Selwyn toured London society together. They visited parties, gaming tables, and horse races, and Montmorency (helped by racing tips picked up by Scarper in the pub) had so much luck in his gambling that burglaries were becoming unnecessary. He did a few, at the homes of some of the more obnoxious members of Bargles, partly to raise the money for club membership (for which he was flattered to have been proposed) and partly to keep his hand in; to prove to himself that he still had the courage, after the horrors of the storm. But otherwise, he was enjoying the pleasures he had set his heart on and the company of his carefree friend.

33. $\mathcal{A}$T THE RACES

Fox-Selwyn's cook could rustle up a splendid picnic at minimal notice. She had known him since he was a child and seen him inherit his father's enthusiasm for last-minute excursions when the weather was fine or life in town started to pall. Her larder was packed with little jars of homemade preserves, pickles, and mustards. Cold meat pies, well wrapped against the air and insects, stood ready on cool stone shelves well away from the light. There were always bottles of fine wine in the cellar. Local tradesmen would rush around with deliveries of quail eggs, smoked fish, salad, and fresh fruit as soon as the errand boy arrived with a note. From a standing start, Cook could pack a sumptuous lunch into wicker hampers within an hour. The starched, white tablecloths, silver cutlery, and crystal glasses were always at the ready, stowed for the next outing as they emerged from the wash after the last one. The very last item, lovingly added just before departure, was always a glassy slab of Cook's own dark brown toffee, wrapped in waxed paper with a little silver hammer alongside so that Fox-Selwyn could smash it into sharp pieces himself. Ever since he had been a little boy he had regarded this "Lockjaw" as the highlight of a picnic, the sweet juice dribbling from his over-full mouth and down his face as he struggled to force his teeth apart. Once the hampers were packed, Fox-Selwyn's manservant, Chivers, would pack them into the carriage, ready for a day out in the country.

Montmorency was lying flat out on the grass beside Sandown Park racetracks, his hat balanced over his eyes to protect them from the fierce sun. With a monogrammed linen napkin, Fox-Selwyn was flapping at the wasps buzzing around his beard. Through the toffee slurps, he gave his views on the horses and riders for the next race. Chivers stood at a discreet distance, ready to refill their glasses, waiting for his instructions about where to place their bets and longing for the chance to get his own small stake on Dandy Darling, which Cook's brother (who knew a man who drank with the jockeys) had told him was a sure thing. Montmorency felt a shadow fall across his body, looked up from under the rim of his hat, and saw cigar ash falling onto the grass at his side. High above him was the silhouette of a man holding a large glass of beer. He spoke with the unmistakable overrefined tone of someone trying to cover up a Birmingham accent. "I say, you two. Well met! Well met, indeed! Half of Bargles seems to be here. Can't be anyone left at the old place, don't you think?"

Montmorency felt his friend Fox-Selwyn stiffen in disgust at the arrival of this intruder. It was Sir Gordon Pewley, a fabulously rich industrialist, who had won membership of Bargles despite Fox-Selwyn's contempt for him (his lordship having been indisposed in "Ploppers," thanks to overindulgence in seafood and champagne on the night of the crucial vote). Pewley owned some of the biggest steelworks in the country. He had been knighted a short time ago, in recognition of his involvement in several major public projects, from each of which his business had benefited hugely. With those profits he had bought the estates of aristocrats who had fallen on hard times. It was said that he was about to demolish a Jacobean mansion in Northamptonshire, to rebuild it in the style of St. Pancras Station. Fox-Selwyn had stayed there as a boy. He did not approve.

"I say," said Pewley, "what do you say to Howling Wolf in the three-thirty? Should be lucky for you. Fox ... Wolf ... Fox-Selwyn ..." His voice trailed off into a rasping laugh and phlegmy cough as he congratulated himself on his little joke, squeaking, "Oh, dear. Oh, dearie me!"

Fox-Selwyn did not like Pewley's overfamiliarity. He did not like wildlife jokes about his name. At school, he had been nicknamed "Wolfman," and jokers had made howling noises in the dark dormitory at night. Somehow, now, in the heat of the afternoon, Fox-Selwyn was back in prep school mood and couldn't resist "accidentally" sticking out his foot as Pewley passed. Sir Gordon toppled and cried out in a distinctly Midlands voice as he crashed onto the grass. His beer sloshed down onto Montmorency, drenching his clothes with its stinking foam.

Chivers was there in an instant with a towel for his master's guest. "I'll get you a clean shirt, sir," he said. "I keep a spare in the carriage for his lordship, in case of such mishaps, sir."

Fox-Selwyn nodded his approval of his manservant's quick thinking, dispatched the wheezing Pewley with a dismissive, "You'd better get off if you're going to bet on that horse," and then turned to help his friend. Montmorency peeled off the soaking shirt, more amused than angry, and glad that Chivers had come so well prepared.

It was then that Fox-Selwyn noticed the scars on his companion's body. He was about to comment on them, when he sensed that he had seen that intricate pattern before. Montmorency caught the puzzled look in his eyes, and fell back on the formula that had worked with the tailor.

"You should have seen the other fellow!"

As Chivers arrived with the clean shirt, Fox-Selwyn joined his friend in embarrassed laughter, and decided to say no more about it. He didn't want to risk spoiling what had been, despite Pewley's intervention, a highly congenial afternoon. So they packed Chivers off with their bets and took their places to watch Dandy Darling romp home.

The friendship of frivolity and fun continued for the rest of the summer. So it was quite a shock for Montmorency when Fox-Selwyn took him into Plotters one evening for their first serious conversation. He was entering yet another new world. A world of international intrigue and danger.

34. $\mathscr{F}$OX-SELWYN AND THE MAURAMANIANS

Fox-Selwyn had lured Montmorency into the tiny room on the pretext of trying out some whisky from his brother's estate in Scotland. Montmorency, who had drunk only beer in his youth, and had taken a while to get used to wine and champagne, had been surprised to find how many different flavors whisky encompassed. The previous night, Fox-Selwyn had introduced him to a peaty malt from the Isle of Skye, with a warm, earthy, almost sickly taste. Montmorency had had to force it down at first, but by the end of the evening he was longing for more. Tonight's tipple was a lighter golden color. The waiter carried the crystal decanter in on a silver tray with two glasses and a little jug of water.

"Just leave it here, Sam. And hide the other bottles. I don't want that rabble out there getting their hands on this. As far as I know we have the only case of it in London."

"Certainly, my lord. But I have a message for you. Sir Gordon Pewley sends his compliments and asks if you would care to join him for a game of cards in Drinks Major."

"No, we have more important business to do here." (The waiter, a true professional, managed to smother a smile.) "Make sure you close the door behind you."

Montmorency and Fox-Selwyn were both already a little drunk. There was nothing new in that, but while Montmorency habitually kept an eye on himself when he was in that condition, Fox-Selwyn was usually more open and exuberant. Tonight he was different. Snuggled into Plotters (a small compartment with no more than a high-backed red velvet bench and a table) he was quiet. Once they were alone, Fox-Selwyn leaned close, and Montmorency could smell the cigars and champagne from earlier in the evening as his friend poured out the whisky.

"Now, see what you think of this. They've been making it up in Banffshire for years, but most of it goes to be blended into other brands. Damned hard to get hold of down here, I can tell you."

Montmorency raised the tumbler to his nose. The powerful fumes hit the back of his throat as harshly as the stench of sewer water.

"Can you smell the barley?" asked Fox-Selwyn.

Montmorency had no idea what barley smelled like, and tried to look as if he was still making up his mind. "I think I'll add a little water," he said, anxious to dilute the fiery liquid.

"Just a touch now. You don't want to drown it. Now, drink it slowly, and tell me what you think."

Montmorency swilled the whisky around in the glass. He sniffed and sipped at it, wondering how to put his indifference about the special drink into polite words. He was about to speak when Fox-Selwyn interrupted him with a surprise announcement, completely off the subject.

"I'm going to tell you something shocking," he whispered huskily.

There was a pause, giving Montmorency time to imagine a panoply of grotesque possibilities.

"I've got a job."

At first Montmorency thought this must be the start of a joke, like the one about the vicar and the umbrella that Fox-Selwyn was given to repeating endlessly when the worse for wear, but he continued solemnly, struggling hard to fish his words out of the drink.

"Don't worry, they don't pay me for it...."

Fox-Selwyn went on to explain that the foreign secretary, who was an old school friend, kept in touch with him, taking an interest in his international travels and from time to time asking him to help out with tasks too sensitive to be done openly by the government. He drew even closer to Montmorency, and added in a dramatic whisper, "This is such a time!"

There was another pause, as Montmorency, relieved that they were off the subject of whisky, racked his brains to think what Fox-Selwyn could be talking about.

"Have you heard of Mauramania?"

For once, Montmorency was glad that he had spent so much time holed up in the Marimion Hotel, reading newspapers. Mauramania wasn't exactly a hot topic in Scarper's pubs and certainly hadn't featured in what little formal education he had received, but he knew now that it was a particularly unstable country at the heart of the Balkans. He listened hard, staring into his whisky (which seemed a little more palatable with every sip).

"The foreign secretary is convinced that the Mauramanians are up to something. There's been a huge influx of new staff at their embassy here. They've sacked all the British people who worked for them, right down to the cleaners. We had a man in there as a gardener, and he says the ambassador is planning to use London as a base for sending guns and explosives to rebels in Mauramania, and to Mauramanian exiles all over Europe."

"But he's their ambassador. Why would he want to do that?"

"Apparently, the plan is to overthrow the King and install the ambassador's brother as president."

Montmorency was having a little trouble keeping up, but Fox-Selwyn carried on. "The trouble is, the king of Mauramania is related to just about every other crowned head you can think of, and if he's deposed, they'll all pile in to restore him. The ones who aren't his family hate him, and they'll fight for the new president just as hard. There could be a major European war."

"But it's such a long way away. Can't we just let them get on with it?" said Montmorency, still wanting to treat the whole thing as a bit of a joke, and to get away to the billiard room or even to the card game with the tiresome Sir Gordon. "I thought those Balkan states were fighting one another and changing hands all the time."

Fox-Selwyn kept up his serious tone. "If the rebels are organizing from here, we can't help being involved. They're Republicans, remember, and our Queen is a cousin of the King they want to overthrow. Who's to say they won't attack her to get at him? And if the royalists find out that we have let the rebels organize on our soil, they could turn against us for revenge. There could be fighting here in Britain, where we haven't had a war for more than two hundred years."

"So why don't we just arrest this ambassador?"

"We have no proof against him, and if our suspicions are wrong, we could end up alienating everyone and putting our own diplomats in danger. And once our diplomats are attacked, we will have to defend them. Our only hope is to find out for sure what's going on, and to get the King of Mauramania to recall his ambassador before the rebels are ready to act. Otherwise it could mean hundreds of thousands of deaths, with trouble in every country where the rebels have managed to get organized and armed. Europe might never be the same again."

"Yes, but where do you come in?" asked Montmorency, sipping at the whisky, slightly embarrassed at finding the story a little hard to follow.

"Well, apart from the tip-off from the gardener, the foreign office has drawn a total blank trying to find out what's happening at the embassy. Apparently, the ambassador likes a good party, so they thought of me! They've asked me to try and get him out to dinner, or better still to get myself in there. I've written. I've even been around trying to leave my card. But I just got frozen out by some beefy Mauramanian at the gate. I had a good look around outside. It's completely impregnable. High walls, guards, the lot. If only I could get inside."

Montmorency, despite the alcohol, realized at once that he could help his friend. The sewers would be the perfect route through the embassy's defenses.

Fox-Selwyn continued. "I've thought of climbing in, but the whole wall is patrolled by guards."

Montmorency was on the verge of speaking, but stopped himself, playing with his whisky glass as he contemplated how to explain his unusual skill and knowledge. He realized for the first time how much he had been longing to show off his abilities to someone, how proud he was of what he did, and how exasperated that nobody knew about it.

Fox-Selwyn was still talking. "I went around to look for some overhanging trees. I thought perhaps I could climb up and drop over the wall, but there's nothing there. Only a few saplings that wouldn't take my weight." He then looked up at his friend as if inviting him to speak.

Montmorency was tempted to reveal everything, but realized that Fox-Selwyn might not admire a life of crime and could reject the friendship of a man whose whole identity was founded on a lie. He tried to distract his friend by returning to the whisky.

"Banffshire, you say?"

Fox-Selwyn looked bemused for a moment.

"Oh, the whisky, yes. It's from one of the oldest distilleries in Scotland. Not quite so hefty as last night's, don't you think …?" He would not allow Montmorency to change the subject. "Now, about the embassy. I was wondering about ladders. But I'd have to dress up as some sort of workman. Unlikely to be convincing, don't you think?"

It was almost as if Fox-Selwyn was teasing Montmorency into making an offer to try to get into the embassy himself.

"I could get in." Montmorency could hardly believe he'd said it. Indeed, at first it didn't seem as if Fox-Selwyn had heard him. Perhaps there was no need for him to expose himself to discovery at all.

Fox-Selwyn carried on, "And I just don't see what else I could try...."

Montmorency couldn't resist the challenge. "I could get in!" he said again.

"And time is running short...."

"I bet you I could get in!"

Turning it into a gambling matter finally got his companion's attention.

"What? How?"

"Don't ask me how, but I bet you a thousand pounds that I can do it."

Montmorency had pulled the figure out of the air. He hadn't a hope of paying off a thousand-pound bet. Fox-Selwyn, for whom a thousand pounds was simply the price of a racehorse or two, or the cost of a very bad night at cards, raised the stakes.

"I'd give you fifteen hundred pounds if you come back with useful information."

Montmorency teased him by upping the sum again. "Two thousand pounds for information."

"And proof positive that you've really been there."

"Two thousand pounds it is."

"But only if you do it by the end of the week. The foreign secretary's away shooting in Scotland, and he wants me to report to him when he gets back on Friday morning."

"I'll go tomorrow night and see you back here on Thursday."

"You're mad."

"I know."

"You're on." Fox-Selwyn reached for the decanter and finally poured himself a glass, refilling Montmorency's. "Here, let's seal the bet in the Water of Life!"

To Montmorency's surprise, Fox-Selwyn didn't attempt to find out how he was going to accomplish his task. He was back on the subject of the whisky, with poetic descriptions of the Banffshire countryside and of his brother's estate, which he said they should visit together one day. It was almost as if he realized that Montmorency didn't want to answer too many questions. It was only years later, long after Fox-Selwyn's brave and bloody death in the service of his country, that Montmorency wondered whether his friend really had been so very drunk that night. He hadn't once stumbled over the pronunciation of Mauramania.

Some people can't even say it when they're sober.

35 SCOUTING

Montmorency wanted to act straightaway. He was excited by the bet, but more important terrified at the prospect of war. He was shocked, too, by the thought that he was in a unique position to do something about that threat: That after all his thieving and loose living, he might actually be about to use his skill and knowledge to do something that would benefit someone other than himself. It was an unfamiliar feeling, for which he didn't have a name. Perhaps it was a kind of pride, the sort he had read about in books, but never really understood until that night. He didn't sleep well, lying in his bed at the Marimion, planning out his assault on the embassy. At first, he was for setting out that night, but he realized that he would have to do some careful research if he was not to risk disaster. The chance of failure was great enough even if he was fully prepared. The potential consequences of a mistake were deadly, not just for him, but for countless others. He would have to stay calm, and go carefully.

The area around the embassy was unfamiliar to Montmorency, and the next afternoon he took a stroll to Kensington to get his bearings, noting the building's precise location in relation to its neighbors, and looking out for any landmarks such as street drains and manholes that might help him position himself accurately underground. From the corner of the main road (which he believed to be above an intersection with the main sewer) there was a line of grand buildings, each with its own grounds. All were institutional and most of them, embassies.

The Mauramanians were roughly in the middle of the row, between the Beneravian embassy and the United Gentlewomen's Society for the Promotion of Bible Studies. All the buildings were set well back from the street. Montmorency reckoned that each would have its own drainage shaft, but that they probably linked up as they ran down to meet the big tunnel. He would have to pace out the area to estimate where the junctions might be. Even then, a lot of guesswork would be involved in finding exactly which pipe led to the Mauramanian embassy itself.

His success on the London scene was a good cover for his presence there. No Mauramanian looking out for spies would have regarded his behavior as at all strange. He met several acquaintances promenading up and down the fashionable street, and quite naturally stopped to talk. Occasionally, he would change direction, exchanging small talk with passersby as he double-checked the precise distances that would be involved in his underground journey into the embassy. He enjoyed the walk and was most amused to be avoided by Sir Clarence Moody, arm in arm with someone far too young and pretty to be Lady Moody (whose nagging and bodily repulsiveness were her husband's favorite subject at Bargles).

Suddenly, he wanted to run. Coming towards him was an image of himself. The same walk, down to the slightly out-turned feet, the left arm behind the back, the head held identically, with the hat tilted slightly to the side. As the figure approached, Montmorency realized it wasn't a copy. This was the original. It was Robert Farcett. The doctor couldn't be avoided. To turn away now would be to draw attention to himself, and here, right outside the embassy gate, Montmorency was determined to pass unnoticed. The two men caught each other's eyes. Montmorency stepped to the side to let the doctor pass, but Farcett had done the same, and they were forced into a mumbling acknowledgment of each other's courtesy. A flash of half recognition lit Farcett's face, and his hand moved towards the brim of his hat. Then he glanced shyly sideways, as if to mask that he had made a mistake, or that he couldn't put a name to the face and didn't want to stop, speak, and reveal his embarrassment. Montmorency gave the tiniest of nods, and they passed each other.

It was over. Even Doctor Farcett didn't know him now. Montmorency's transformation was complete.

36. INTO THE FORTRESS

Later, in Scarper's room, back in his own skin and the clothes that matched it, Montmorency felt out of place. He'd been wondering for some time if he even liked Scarper anymore, and whether he could find some way of removing him from his life. But not today. He needed Scarper for the biggest job of his career: the first that was for something more important than his own enrichment. Yet, in these clothes and making preparations to go back into the sewers, the thought of Fox-Selwyn's bet loomed as large as the prospect of saving Europe. Montmorency wasn't proud of the feeling, but if Scarper needed the prospect of a two-thousand-pound reward to motivate him, so be it.

He checked his kit. It was time to go. Scarper was in charge now. He was the one with the skill for the task, and this one would need all his knowledge of that underground world. The first part of the journey was routine, but near the embassy itself he had to match the underground features with the memory of his walk, and he was faced with a fan of small tunnels and chutes, remnants of old drains built long before Bazalgette's network — smaller and slimier than the ones Scarper was used to, with crumbling sides in place of Bazalgette's sturdy bricks.

Scarper clambered and slithered his way along the unfamiliar shafts. Then, when he knew he must be within yards of his goal, he was faced with a choice of routes. He dithered about which to take, but the decision was made for him seconds later when the left-hand opening disgorged a flood of steaming foam. Memories of the storm came with it, and he forced himself up into the relative safety of the right-hand branch, which climbed steeply towards a dim light.

The shaft was narrow. He could move along only by wedging his elbows and knees against the sides and hauling his body forward, terrified of getting stuck, or of dropping back down and having to climb again. At last he reached the metal grille that topped off the shaft. He took off his waders and tied them together, hooking them to the underside of the grating. Then, as he raised his head to look through the bars, two large feet settled on top and stayed there for a very long time. Scarper froze, expecting at any moment to have filthy water poured down onto his head. Instead, all he got was a cigarette butt and then the feet disappeared. Moments later a door banged shut, and Scarper risked raising the grille.

To his relief, it gave way to a push from his shoulder, and looking around in the gloom he could see that he was in a courtyard. From the direction of the slamming door came the clatter of a kitchen and an incomprehensible hubbub of foreign male voices. He could be pretty sure this wasn't the United Gentlewomen's Society for the Promotion of Bible Studies. But were those words Mauramanian or Beneravian? No time to find out now. Scarper launched himself from the hole and scuttled into the shadows. Almost immediately the door burst open again and a sweaty, hairy man nipped over and casually peed down the drain. Scarper definitely wasn't with the United Gentlewomen. He slid in through the open door and hid under the sink.

The kitchen was a long, narrow room with a huge table running down the middle. On either side, lines of cooks in bloody aprons were skinning, chopping, and slicing, and regularly chucking handfuls of peelings and cast-off gristle into putrid buckets on the floor. Every now and then they reached up to a vast iron frame suspended from the ceiling, from which dangled pots, strainers, ladles, and other kitchen tools. There was an air of grumpy industry and a smell of foreign food from the bubbling pots on the opposite wall.

At one end of the room a door stood open, and from his hideout, crouched under the draining board, Scarper could see a narrow corridor, where some of the cooks were changing from their spattered gear into embroidered jerkins, tight knee-length breeches, and fancy velvet slippers. They must be the waiters. It was going to be quite a feast. Across the hall another door opened into the dining room. A grand table was being laid. The stiff cloth hung down right to the floor, heavy with woven designs of flowers, fruit, and fantastic beasts around the edge. Two of the uniformed servants were carefully counting out cutlery from elaborate wooden boxes, inlaid with mother-of-pearl. He had to get into that dining room, but how?

Against his hip he could feel the weight of the heavy iron hook he used to raise his manhole cover in Covent Garden. Looking across the kitchen, through the forest of legs in front of him, he could see a line of highly polished silver platters leaning against the wall, ready to be piled with food and hoisted up on to the waiters' shoulders. Scarper took his hook and flung it towards them, hoping that he wouldn't hit one of the cooks on the way. It struck the first tray, and the whole line collapsed like a row of dominoes, clattering and spinning amid an explosion of curses. The waiters from across the way ran in to see what was happening. For an instant, Scarper's path was clear, and he shuffled and rolled into the dining room and under the table. All he could do now was wait and hope that he was with the Mauramanians, and not the Beneravians. Lying there on the floor, he was electrified by this new level of danger. Scared but thrilled by the prospect of being caught; physically enjoying his panic and the need to overlay it with a calm that might save his life. This was the feeling that kept him returning to the sewers time and time again despite the comfortable gentility of his new life. At moments like this, being Scarper was just as much fun as being Montmorency.

The cutlery counters came back quickly; laughing at first, then clearly irritated that they had lost track of their task and would have to start all over again. When they had counted the cutlery, they set to work on the plates, side plates, soup plates, candlesticks, and dishes of all types.

Whatever language this is, Scarper joked to himself, *I'll be fluent in the numbers before tonight is over!*

37. DINNER

Lying under the table, even surrounded by so much finery, was not unlike being in his prison cell, and he drew on the reserves of patience he had cultivated there to deal with the wait. He didn't know how long he would be trapped, silent and unable to move. All the time he was observing his surroundings, peeping under the cloth to get some idea of the geography of the room, listening to the footfalls of the waiters as they transformed the scene with increasing bustle and anxiety. Through the thin slice of light at the bottom of the tablecloth, he had to plan escape routes. Even the smallest detail might save his life if he were discovered.

He still couldn't be certain where he was. He imagined the fun Fox-Selwyn would have with him when he heard that he'd broken into the wrong embassy. Even if it was the right place, exactly what information would he be taking back for the foreign secretary? News of a spectacularly greasy kitchen and a description of the underside of a huge tablecloth were hardly likely to save Europe. He had to find something worth reporting. Once or twice he thought he caught the word "Mauramania" amid the mumbling babble of the strange language; but even if he were right, that didn't prove anything. It could just be the Beneravians talking about their next-door neighbors. Perhaps the exotic phrases wouldn't translate into an heroic musing on Republicanism, but would turn out to be some mundane piece of Balkan rivalry. "We'll show those stinking Mauramanians how to give a party. No one can outdo Beneravia when it comes to boiling a beetroot into oblivion!"

He tried a few more fantasy translations, all the time scanning the small gap between the floor and the bottom of the tablecloth. A new voice had entered the mix, barking orders as its owner made a circuit of the table. The waiters lined up behind the chairs, ready to pull them back when the guests took their places. There was some last-minute shuffling and relighting of spluttering candles. Then suddenly silence, a pause, and the sound of the wide double doors at the end of the room swinging open to let in several pairs of expensive shoes.

Amazingly, someone was speaking English. It was heavily accented English, but cultured and clear. This must be the ambassador.

"So, as you can see, we can still do things in our traditional Mauramanian style, even so far from home!"

"Marvelous, marvelous," came the reply.

The Mauramanians must be entertaining an English guest. Perhaps there was hope of getting some information to take back to Fox-Selwyn after all.

The ambassador took his visitor on a tour of the room. From under the cloth, Scarper could see their four feet followed by a line of others, bunching together as the ambassador stopped at a particular painting or tapestry to tell the story of how it had been acquired for the Mauramanian people. He pointed out historic pieces of furniture, the magnificent carpet and tapestries, portraits of Mauramanian rulers and heroes, and finally the grand table setting, most notable for the splendid Russian cutlery — one of the largest and most ornate sets in Europe. It had been a gift to his own great-grandfather who, like him, had been a diplomat and who had become, while representing his homeland in Moscow, a favorite (perhaps even a lover) of the Empress Catherine the Great.

" I don't think your Queen Victoria will be giving me any spoons!" he added, setting his English guest into a burst of throaty laughter that led to a bout of chesty coughing and then a high-pitched gasping wheeze of, "Oh, dear. Oh, dearie me!"

Scarper knew that laugh. He struggled to recall where he had heard it and listened all the more intently as the party sat down to eat. He wriggled his way to the head of the table where the ambassador and his guest of honor had taken their seats. Farther down the table, the other diners had set up a racket of Mauramanian, but the two at the top continued in English. It was hard to hear what they were saying amid the clatter of plates. All the time, Scarper struggled to identify the owner of the English voice. He knew from the trouser legs poking under the cloth that the man was rich, though the quality of the fabric rather than the style of the cut told him so. This was someone with plenty of money, but no great flair.

Then it came again: that wracking convulsion of a laugh, conjuring up the world of Eats Major and Drinks Minor, and of a sunny day and a beer-soaked shirt at Sandown Park races. It was Sir Gordon Pewley, the big bore from Bargles.

Scarper was mystified. If Fox-Selwyn, an amusing and well-connected figure in London society, couldn't get an invitation to the ambassador's table, what on earth was this uncultured industrialist doing there? Why had the foreign office sent him? The answer came soon enough, and Scarper strained to catch and memorize every word of the deal that was being struck above his head.

Pewley wasn't working for the British government. He was deeply involved in the Mauramanian arms trade and was after a bigger slice. He had his money on the ambassador's brother and wanted to be in at the birth of the Mauramanian republic, whether Queen Victoria's ministers wanted it or not. And Sir Gordon knew they didn't want it. As he told the ambassador in great detail, he'd had a private meeting with the foreign secretary only two weeks ago and was now in the happy position of being able to pass on the full details of the British government's most secret plans.

As Scarper listened, two worries impinged on his excitement and pride. How was he going to get out? And how would he ever be able to prove to Fox-Selwyn that he really had been present tonight? The story was too momentous to be believed. Fox-Selwyn would think he had made it up. He had to find some material thing to demonstrate his credibility, but what? He could hardly bite off a bit of tablecloth and expect his friend to know where it had come from. Perhaps a candlestick would do, but no doubt the ambassador and his staff would be keeping an eye on those — especially with a crook like Sir Gordon Pewley in the room.

His thoughts were interrupted by a clattering to Pewley's left. The lady sitting there (presumably the ambassador's wife) had dropped her fork. As she must have known better than anyone else, this wasn't just any fork, but a precious family heirloom. She started shuffling around, trying to find it with her feet. Her dainty silken slippers skipped about like a ballerina's, discreetly at first, then with more and more urgency, though all the time she seemed calm and controlled from her bottom up. Scarper was thrilled. Here was his chance. It would be the perfect souvenir of the evening. He reached out to grab the fork just as the woman tracked it down, dragged it towards her with one foot, and started sliding it delicately up the inside of her other calf. When her hand came down to collect it, it brushed Sir Gordon Pewley's leg. He responded with a squeeze of her knee. She stiffened in disgust, and the fork fell. As Scarper pocketed it, her feet crashed flat to the floor and she stood, knocking her chair backward, screaming Mauramanian curses that didn't need translation. There was the sound of a slap and a spluttering cough. All around the table, guests rose and left their places to see the cause of the trouble.

No one noticed Scarper retracing his crouching roll into the kitchen, and no one was looking in his direction as he lifted the grille on the courtyard drain. He was back in Covent Garden by eleven, and running a bath for Montmorency at the Marimion before midnight.

38. REPORTING BACK

Montmorency contemplated writing down the story for Fox-Selwyn, but he wasn't sure if his handwriting was up to it. Although he'd been practicing, the longest thing he had ever written was that first letter of instructions to the Marimion. Any slips in telling this complex tale might make it seem like his own invention. So, sitting in Plotters the next day, he told his friend that in his view the information was too sensitive to be committed to paper. That at least got Fox-Selwyn's attention. That and the fork, which Montmorency pulled from his dinner jacket with a flourish. It was a remarkable object. The prongs were the only similarity it bore to any fork Montmorency had ever seen, and even they were engraved with a swirling design of intense intricacy. The shaft was tooled gold, surrounding a minute, brightly colored enamel picture of a shepherd boy blowing a pipe. The detail would have been impressive in an object ten times the size.

Fox-Selwyn had heard of the ambassador's ancestor and his intimate relationship with Empress Catherine. He believed his friend's extraordinary tale.

"Some poor soul in the kitchen will have paid a high price when they discovered that fork was missing. Will have lost his job. Or worse." Fox-Selwyn dragged a finger across his throat and rolled his eyes to emphasize his point, and Montmorency felt an unfamiliar glimmer of guilt about the theft.

The next morning, Fox-Selwyn arrived at the Marimion in his carriage to collect Montmorency for their trip to the foreign office. Cissie, who was rearranging an ugly vase of orange dahlias in the hotel lobby, was intrigued to see so eminent a visitor at such an early hour. She curtsied shyly and then, remembering all the details from her concerted study of magazines, astounded him with intimate inquiries about the health and whereabouts of several of his relations. Her father, remarking to himself (not for the first time) how Scarper was never around when you needed him, climbed the grand staircase to tell Montmorency that he was wanted downstairs. Montmorency emerged wearing one of Mr. Lyons's most fashionable new suits, and Cissie admired him more than ever. She took his failure to acknowledge her in front of his noble friend as a discreet affirmation of their growing (though secret) love. In fact, he hadn't even noticed she was there in his anxiety to reach the foreign office without delay.

Convincing the foreign secretary of Montmorency's story proved harder than Montmorency or Fox-Selwyn had expected. He had been to parties at Sir Gordon Pewley's house and had quietly accepted a loan from him when the lifestyle demanded by his job started to strain the family purse. He didn't want to think badly of his benefactor or to suffer from his association with him. Once again the fork did the trick. The foreign secretary had dined at the embassy shortly after the new ambassador's arrival in Britain. He had actually eaten with one just like it. So he listened, with his back to Montmorency and Fox-Selwyn, nervously toying with his sideburns as he gazed from his tall office window across the lawns and ponds of St. James's Park. Once he was persuaded that what Montmorency said was true, he made him hand over the fork. It was to be kept as evidence, said the foreign secretary. Montmorency had his doubts, and imagined it would be brought out at family gatherings in years to come, as the old politician told and retold his own version of its (and his) part in securing world peace. He was sorry to see the fork go. He knew it was too valuable and recognizable to be sold, but he had a growing stock of sentimental souvenirs under the floorboards in Scarper's room, and felt its rightful place was among them, along with Professor Humbley's valuable book, which Montmorency saw as a symbol of his failure to resist the lure of crime and which even Scarper had been too ashamed to sell.

"I will have to make some checks with embassies and agents abroad," said the foreign secretary. "I need hardly say that this is a matter of the utmost secrecy. You must not speak of it to anyone, and above all you must give no indication to Sir Gordon that he is under surveillance."

So Montmorency and Fox-Selwyn had to put up with Pewley's self-regarding pomposity at Bargles for a little while longer. They even played cards with him that evening, observing both that he cheated and that he gossiped freely about his friendship with several members of the royal family. Even Montmorency found that a bit vulgar, and Fox-Selwyn was scandalized by the indiscretion of it. Montmorency noticed a slight bruise on Sir Gordon's left cheek. That must have been where the ambassador's wife had landed her slap after his ill-advised grope under the tablecloth. Fox-Selwyn ordered more and more drink for the traitorous bore, reasoning that it was better to render him incapacitated than to run the risk of him alerting his Mauramanian connections to even the tiniest whiff of suspicion.

Sir Gordon managed to spill some alcohol over Montmorency again. It was brandy this time. Pewley thought it was a terrific joke. "Oh, dear. Oh, dearie me!" he chortled, descending into one of his great coughing fits, and hawking up a gob of spit into a flowerpot.

When Montmorency had heaved him into a cab and sent him home semiconscious, he found himself wiping his fingers with his handkerchief as if to rid himself of some noxious contagion, just as one of the members of the Scientific Society had done after handling his own body five years before.

It was weeks before the foreign office had made all the necessary checks on Montmorency's story, consulting embassies and consuls all over Europe to coordinate raids on the Mauramanian rebels. Meanwhile, undercover policemen secretly followed Sir Gordon Pewley around to his London contacts, gathering enough evidence to justify his arrest. Fox-Selwyn was kept up to date on what was happening, on the strict understanding that he should tell no one in case the counterplot leaked out and triggered an early coup against the Mauramanian king. Montmorency could only trust his friend's coded assurances that everything was under control, and wait until he could be fully informed. He suspected that he was being watched himself and, despite temptation, lived a blameless life during that agonizing period of waiting.

Eventually, he was sent a message requiring his attendance upon the foreign secretary in Whitehall. It gave him quite a thrill to enter the nerve center of the empire, though he wasn't much taken with the classical plainness of the building's exterior, preferring the chaotic splendor of the Houses of Parliament across the road.

Inside, the foreign secretary explained to him about the continuing investigation of Sir Gordon Pewley, and impressed on him the need to avoid doing or saying anything that might tip him off in the days to come. He had been speaking for some time — about how grateful the Mauramanian government was, and how war would certainly be avoided — before Montmorency realized that he was being offered a job. It would be the sort of work Fox-Selwyn had confessed to, though in Montmorency's case it would be paid.

He discussed the offer with Fox-Selwyn in Plotters, hinting that he would be reluctant to give up his present way of life, but resisting the strong temptation to tell him exactly where he was from and what he had been up to. In the end he left the decision to a cut of the cards, and when Fox-Selwyn turned up the queen of spades, Montmorency was set for a career of travel and espionage in the service of his country.

39. REPARATIONS

And so, in the morning, Scarper could be swept out of Montmorency's life. He dressed in his servant's smartest clothes and took off for Covent Garden. Vi was on the step in her petticoat, fiercely combing out last night's tangles from her hair. She gave him a warm smile. He realized that he had become quite fond of her and might even miss her.

His little room was hardly changed from the day he had moved in. The damp patch was bigger, and there were more and better clothes draped across the back of the chair. A cardboard box in the corner held spare lamps, string, sacks, and other paraphernalia he had picked up, thinking it might come in handy down the sewers. A couple of old newspapers lined the cavity under the floor where the last of his booty was hidden. That first article, which had so infuriated Sergeant Newman, was there alongside one describing Freakshow's execution. Odd pages wrapped up jewelry and knickknacks from his raids. There were some things he hadn't been able to sell because they were too valuable, and others that had turned out to be almost worthless once examined in the light. A few he hadn't wanted to part with for sentimental reasons, like the watch that had been in his pocket throughout the ordeal of the storm. It was smashed and useless, but was miraculously still there when he had come to from his near drowning — a testament to the honesty of the boatmen who had brought him home. One or two things he had been too ashamed to sell once he'd read of their owners' grief at their loss. Still more he had forgotten about entirely, particularly those acquired in the later days of his career when Scarper was at the height of his abilities, but was often delivered to work by Montmorency far too drunk to concentrate on what he was taking or on where he put it. He gathered up the loot from under the floor and stuffed it into one of the sacks. With the floorboards still up, he sat on the edge of the creaky bed and read once more the account of Freakshow's trial. He screwed it into a ball ready to throw it away, then straightened it out again, folded it, and put it in his pocket. It would be best to have something to remind him of the man who had taught him so many of his skills and had taken the blame for so many of his crimes.

Suddenly, there was a rustling and panting at the door. Scarper slotted back the loose boards over the hole just as Mrs. Evans walloped into the room. She took in his confusion, saw the sack, and realized what was going on.

"Flitting?"

"Getting ready to go, yes," he said, trying not to look thrown.

"I … I … I …," she stuttered, groping for something to say. "I was just going to change your sheets."

Scarper smiled. As far as he could tell, the same graying tatters had been on the bed since the day he had arrived more than two years before.

"Really?" he said, trying not to laugh.

"Well, it's probably about time."

Scarper realized she was a little uncomfortable herself. She, too, had been planning something out of the ordinary.

"Only it's just that Vi an' me …," she babbled in embarrassment. "We was wondering if you'd like to come out for a drink.

It's just that you've been here a while now, and you're always so good about the rent, and we was just wondering ..."

"What a shame I have to go."

"Well, ain't that typical of Vi an' me. Bad timing as usual."

"I really can't stay. Got to get going."

"I'll have to get someone else for the room," she said with a sigh, halfheartedly rubbing some dust from the table with her sleeve.

"Well, here's a little something in case you can't find anyone straightaway." He pressed two weeks' rent money into her hand.

"You had a spot of luck then, dearie?"

"Something like that. I'd better be on my way." And he took her by the arm and helped her down the stairs.

Vi was at the door beaming up towards them, assuming they were off to the pub, and Scarper was saddened and surprised by the drop in her spirits when she heard he was going away. They spent longer saying good-bye than they had ever spent together during his time living under their roof. As he set off there were even teardrops on Vi's cheeks, and after dabbing them with the edge of her petticoat, she used the damp cloth to wipe the "No" off the "Vakensees" sign. After a few steps, Scarper turned back to Mrs. Evans. "Perhaps you might as well see to those sheets after all," he shouted with a wave.

At the Marimion, he took the back staircase for the last time. The ever-changing team of chambermaids and porters were going about their business as on any ordinary day, and most of them greeted him with little more than a casual nod. He dropped into the kitchen, where the sulky chef was introducing yet another new deputy to the mysteries of the hotel menu. One long-serving pot-boy threw him a piece of carrot, which he accepted with a smile and a wave. On the way out, he couldn't resist a last snarl at Cissie, who was picking at the leftovers on the breakfast trays.

She sneered back, unaware that she would never see him again. In Montmorency's room, he changed his clothes and folded Scarper away forever.

Leaving the Marimion was more of an enterprise than quitting Covent Garden. Montmorency was staggered at the amount of possessions he had acquired during his stay. He had to buy luggage for transporting it all, and the hotel arranged a special van to take it to Bargles, where he was to take up residence in one of the bedrooms on the top floor. Cissie was distraught. She wept every day until the duke of Cumberland's cousin's wife's nephew came to stay.

In Covent Garden, Scarper's departure had made an even greater impact than he knew. In his hurry to get Mrs. Evans out of his room, he had missed a few bits of jewelry from his stash under the floorboards. Months later, the new tenant — a dancer — was practicing her pirouettes and brought down the ceiling in the room below. Vi heard the crash and went up to inspect the damage. She believed in miracles from the moment she found the gems lying among the dust and splinters. She wore the diamond necklace once, on one of her nights outside the opera, but her mother couldn't resist the urge to sell it, even though, on the black market, it fetched much less than its real value. They meant to spend the money wisely, but somehow it all vanished on drink and clothes, and the gold bracelet and emerald ring went the same way not long afterward. The fence who bought them was later arrested. The jewels were identified as coming from one of a series of unsolved raids that had taken place after the hanging of "The Hopping Horror." Despite the fence's protestations of innocence, Sergeant Newman managed to pin all similar unresolved cases on the unfortunate man, and any risk of inquiries into Scarper's old activities was lifted.

With Scarper gone, Montmorency found himself acting in unusual ways. On Wednesday afternoon he took a cab to Holland Park, to leave Robert Farcett's big bag, complete with its original contents and the impossible cuff links, just inside the doctor's (still unlocked) study windows. He had at last realized who must have given him the mysterious envelope he never had the chance to open when he left prison. Perhaps Doctor Farcett had sent some money to recompense him for the indignities he had suffered in the cause of furthering his career. Perhaps he had written an address where he could be contacted, so that 493's progress could still be monitored, documented, and illustrated for the medical profession. Perhaps he had simply wanted to stay in touch, having developed an affection for his patient, and an interest in his physical and moral survival. What must he have thought when 493 failed to make contact? He could hardly have suspected the truth: that a prison guard had drunk away the money and laughed with his fellows at the sentimentality of the letter that had accompanied it.

There was no sign of life at Robert Farcett's house that day, and Montmorency sidled in and out of the garden without fear of detection. He didn't notice that the doctor was in the conservatory, talking with his new patient and friend, Lord George Fox-Selwyn. Farcett was showing Fox-Selwyn a rare plant that one of his friends in the Scientific Society had brought back from a recent trip abroad. It was a fragile seedling, but if it grew, it should produce leaves with the power to kill pain and induce sleep. Farcett was hoping he could find a way to distill the essence of the sap, so that it could be compounded into a handy pill or syrup. The two men looked up as they heard a rustle in the bushes. They both thought there was something familiar about the figure disappearing through the gate at the other end of the garden, but though they ran out to catch him, they failed. Back inside the study, Farcett found the bag and identified it and its contents as possessions that had gone missing some two years before. Fox-Selwyn recognized the cufflinks and the jacket, but said nothing. He looked up at the diagram of 493 and his wounds. The scars were as he remembered them from the day at the races. He welcomed the confirmation that he had been right to back his hunch about the unusual talents and essential goodness of his friend Montmorency. Perhaps one day he would tell Montmorency what he thought he knew. Perhaps one day he would take Farcett into his confidence.

But now he noticed that the doctor's initial shock at discovering his old clothes had been replaced by confusion and remorse.

"I must find her," whispered Farcett.

Fox-Selwyn didn't understand. This was the last reaction he had expected.

"Elizabeth, my maid. I dismissed her when these things went missing. I thought her negligent or, worse, dishonest. I have wronged her. I must find her and put things right."

"I will help you," said Fox-Selwyn, relieved and moved that Farcett's immediate concern was for justice for his employee rather than to find the identity of the mysterious man in the garden.

The next morning someone else was bemused by a bag of clothes. The old tramp who still slept each night on the steps of the theater in Drury Lane woke to find several sets of smart work clothes in a sack by his side. They were Scarper's, of course. Some were a little smelly, but others were more than respectable. With winter setting in they would be useful. He had quite forgotten the clothes that had been stolen as he slept so long before.

At Horatio House in Nelson Place, Professor Humbley, who had been up all night writing about the mysterious workings of the human heart and mind, heard a tap on his front door.

There was nobody to be seen, but on the step lay his lost copy of Plutarch, now inscribed: *To a great man, kind and good. With thanks.* It was unsigned.

That same morning, Sir Gordon Pewley noticed that a valuable silver clock was missing from his drawing room mantelpiece. He was the final victim of Scarper's skills in breaking and entering. He sent for the police to report his loss, but when they came it was to take him into custody, to the very jail where Scarper had been born and where Montmorency's new life had begun.

Pewley was defeated by the convict's life. His nerves and stamina collapsed, and he spent many a night in the infirmary, under the malevolent gaze of Marston the guard. These days Marston liked to boast of how he had subdued "The Hopping Horror" during his time at the jail. Other convicts said they couldn't understand how the man they had known as Freakshow had turned into such a monster, if indeed he really had. Barney Watts, still inside, still snarling and mean, claimed to have taught the "Horror" everything he knew.

Nurse Darnley saw a lot of Pewley in the bleak hospital room. She tried to forgive him and was as considerate as ever with sips of water and a gentle word after the rigors of a chilly night. But in her heart, she didn't care for his self-pitying whine, and was secretly glad when he was carried off by an infection caused by poor sanitation and the shock of prison food.

The authorities were relieved, too. Sir Gordon's death meant there was no need for a trial, and the full details of the Mauramanian plot could remain a secret. Luckily for the foreign secretary, his loan from the traitor stayed a secret, too. He never had to pay it back, and basked in the goodwill of the prime minister and the Queen, who were jubilant at the way he had solved such a potentially explosive situation so quietly.

And so, Montmorency put another world behind him. Though under the bed in his room at Bargles lay a splendid pair of waders. He told one of the Sams that he was preparing for a fishing trip to Scotland. He told himself that they were souvenirs.

But in his heart he knew why he was keeping them.

Just in case.

ABOUT THE AUTHOR

Eleanor Updale prides herself on writing books that can be enjoyed by readers of all ages. Her *Montmorency* series has won awards on both sides of the Atlantic, including the Blue Peter prize for 'The Book I Couldn't Put Down'. Eleanor was educated at Oxford and London universities, and has a PhD in History. A former TV and radio producer, she is a member of the Clinical Ethics Committee at Great Ormond Street Hospital for Children, and of the UK Donation Ethics Committee. She is also an Associate Fellow of the Royal Literary Fund, a Governor of the children's charity, Coram, and an Ambassador for the Prince's Foundation for Children and the Arts. Her other books include *Johnny Swanson* and *The Last Minute*. She lives in Edinburgh and London.